AGƎNT ASHA

OPERATION CYBER CHOP

SOPHIE DEEN

ILLUSTRATED BY
PRIYANKA SACHDEV

**WALKER
BOOKS**

Prologue

Time: unknown

"It's perfect," Shelly whispered, leaning against a glass wall that slid open onto her balcony. She lived in the tallest skyscraper in London, and the yellow lights of the city twinkled behind her. The sun had set hours ago, and muffled sounds of traffic could be heard in the distance.

Shelly was squinting at the shadowy shape looming in front of her. She could only make out a few jagged edges, but she already knew how big it was. She'd been working on it for four years, and she could barely wait any longer.

Ricardo fumbled around with a few cables

that lay on the floor. "Ready!" he said, excitedly. Shelly pressed a glowing button on her watch, took a sharp breath in and watched a greenish pool of light spread slowly across the room, as the Cyber Oak blinked into life. It was a gigantic tree, but there wasn't so much as a twig's worth of wood in it. From the base of its trunk to the tips of its leaves, it was made entirely of metal, glass and plastic. Small cables ran up it, disappearing like veins into the branches. It was alive with short pulses of light.

Shelly walked around her masterpiece. It looked the same from every angle: each leaf was indistinguishable from the next; every branch was identical. The leaves swayed slowly back and forth, in time with each other. As they moved, Shelly caught a glimpse of the cameras inside.

They were tiny.

"It's stunning." Shelly's fingers tingled. The Cyber Oak was the next piece in her puzzle. She already owned FaceSpace, which everyone used to search the web and talk to their friends. Not to mention the largest shop in the world: the ShellyShop. But parks and green spaces – beautiful public spaces, made for everyone to enjoy – had always been out of reach. Until now, anyway.

Whenever there was a glimmer of sunshine, people flocked outside in groups. Shelly didn't understand why – parks were muddy, flowers were boring and there was nowhere to plug in a laptop. Worst of all, parks had no Internet.

"Once these trees are deployed, we'll be able to watch people all the time. We'll be able to hear their secret conversations and see what they're doing. We'll even be able to smell them!" Shelly clasped her hands together.

"Yes, but—"

"Just imagine how powerful I'll be when we have all that data!" Shelly continued.

"In fact, why wait any longer. It's time to launch."

Ricardo's eyes widened. "Erm, really, Shelly? What about the test results? Won't people in Wembley kick up a fuss? You know, because the Cyber Oaks will destroy local wildlife, and they create so much pollution..."

"Ah, no one will care about that, not when we're giving them WiFi!" Shelly looked like she was swatting a fly away as she spoke. "The truth is what we make of it! Now stop stressing, Rickybae. You know it's bad for your mental health!"

Ricardo smoothed his right eyebrow with his little finger nervously. "It's just ... the climate has been the number one trending issue for years now. People really do care about it. Especially children."

Shelly sighed irritably and looked back out of the window, spotting a recycling van below. She had noticed more of those recently, and a lot more people were posting about the "plastic problem" on social media. Perhaps Ricardo was on to something. Shelly picked up her phone to open FaceSpace and started to mindlessly scroll. A set of headphones caught her eye. The hashtags read: #plasticfree #loveourplanet. The post had 68.2 million likes.

"Who is this little treasure?" Shelly asked, showing Ricardo her screen. An idea had started to form.

"Oh, that's DJ Annie Bestlyfe. She's massive. Last year she was voted 'Sickest Juggler' in the Ibiza DJ wars. Everyone loves her."

Shelly pictured DJ Bestlyfe leaning against a Cyber Oak and taking a selfie.

"She's perfect. Find her and bring her to me."

Chapter 1

-.-. .- -. / -.-- --- ..- / .-. . .- -.. / - .... ..
... ..--..

August 07 – 17:13

Asha was halfway up her favourite tree in
Wembley Park when she remembered why
she wasn't meant to be climbing trees today. It
was Nani-Ji's seventieth birthday and she had
been forced to wear her "smart" clothes. Dad's
instructions had been clear: don't get dirty, don't
argue with your sister and don't burp in public.

She hadn't burped yet or argued with her
sister. But Asha was pretty sure she'd just ripped
her sweater trying to grab a branch overhead.
She wished she was in her super-stretchy, extra-
bouncy all-weather bodysuit. But she only wore

that on top-secret spy missions, not at boring family picnics.

The oak tree Asha was climbing gave her a view right over the park. Down below, Asha could see Nani-Ji waving at her, while Mum, Dad and all her cousins tucked into plates of food.

Asha wanted to climb higher. As she shifted her weight to get a better handhold, a high-pitched

beep startled her. It seemed to be coming from the trunk. She moved a leaf aside and found herself staring straight into a camera lens hidden in the bark. A thin black cable trailed from it. It beeped again.

Who would hide a camera in a tree? And why? Asha leaned

in to look closer. A small heart-like shape was engraved on the camera's surface. Biting the inside of her cheek, Asha traced the cable with her finger, twisting her torso to reach higher up.

"Asha! Chalo! Food's ready!" Dad's voice bellowed across the park.

"In a minute!" Asha yelled, pulling at the camera. It wouldn't budge.

"Now, Rani!" Dad yelled back.

Asha's spy training rushed to the front of her mind: *Think for yourself. Question everything.* If she moved quickly, she might find another clue. She lifted herself onto her tiptoes and continued to trace the cable, but then her right foot slipped on some moss and she lost her balance. Asha instantly tucked herself into the official crash-landing position: a small ball. She hit the ground with a thud, dusted herself off and ran over to her family. She'd have to come back another time, when she was on her own.

"Asha beta, you must slow down!" Nani-Ji fussed over her granddaughter, checking her knees and smoothing her hair. "Remember – one step at a time. Big problem? Make it small steps. Trust your Nani-Ji. Simple trick, works for everything in life." Nani-Ji winked at Asha. In response, Asha squeezed her eyes shut and scrunched up her face. Asha used to do this before she had learned how to wink. Now it was just something she did to make Nani-Ji smile. "Now go and get some food – you're wasting away!" Nani-Ji teased.

Asha walked over to her dad, who was doling out paneer wraps and parathas, and chatting away to cousins, aunties, uncles and friends. His fold-out table was groaning under the weight of all the different dishes.

"It feels like half of Wembley are here," Asha mumbled as Dad served her a dollop of chaat.

"Incorrect. There are currently 37 people at this gathering, but the population of Wembley is approximately 102,856," said Drone. Drone was Asha's nannybot – a flying robot nanny. She was programmed to look after Asha, worry about a gazillion things a day and fact check everything anyone said.

"38, if you include Tumble," Drone added. They turned to look at Tumble, a hamster-like toy Asha had invented when she was six years old. He was on the picnic rug with his tiny phone held out in front of him, trying to get a shot with Nani-Ji.

"What's up, friendos! We're here for the big 7-0, and we've got a picnic for DAYS. Stay tuned for #familytime. Peace and rotis! #Summerfun." Tumble moved around as he spoke to his camera.

"Tumble, put that away! No vlogging while we're eating," said Dad.

Asha tried to push the hidden camera to the back of her mind and plonked herself down next to her big sister, Anushka.

"Nice climbing, Cr-asha!" Nush teased. Nush thought she was too cool to climb anything. "You know, that would never happen with a Cyber Oak. Their branches catch people when they fall, so they are, like, 100 per cent safe, even for babies like you." Nush elbowed Asha. "And they are totally great for the planet too."

Asha had a mouth full of chaat. "If you care so much about the planet, why don't you stop talking about it and actually do something about it," she mumbled.

Nush turned towards her aunties, ignoring Asha. "Did you know the Cyber Oak is 70,000 times more powerful than a normal tree? It can even reverse climate change."

"Really?!" Asha asked. That was a big claim.

"Er, hello! Wakey-wakey! It's all over the news." Nush rolled her eyes.

The residents of Wembley had been given a

month to decide whether to vote "yes" or "no" to the Cyber Oak – the world's first digital tree. If they voted "yes", all of the natural trees in Wembley Park would be replaced with Cyber Oaks. The vote was taking place online at 3 p.m. on Sunday, and Nush had been trying to convince everyone at the picnic to vote "yes". Asha hadn't been following the story as closely. She stared blankly at Nush.

Auntie Meera leaned in. "Your sister is right. Trees are more dangerous than you think."

"Yep, they are super flammable and much too tall." Nush looked around the park. "It's so cool to think that we could have the Cyber Oak right here. I'm psyched."

"God willing!" Auntie Meera nodded enthusiastically. "Just last week, some reporters interviewed your Uncle Nik." Meera winked at her husband, who had his mouth full of jalebi. "Now he thinks he's famous."

Usually, Asha loved anything and everything to do with tech, but she had a funny feeling about the Cyber Oak. She'd been coming to Wembley Park since she was in nappies. It was where she met friends, made dens and buried time capsules. Asha knew each tree like the back of her hand; she loved their knobbly skin and muddy smells, and most of all, she loved climbing them. She'd never told anyone, but Asha thought that trees could feel things. It made her sad to think they would be chopped down. And where would dogs wee?

"In my day, trees were fine just as they were." Nani-Ji raised her eyebrows. "How can a tree be bad? They clean the air. The Cyber Oak is nonsense!"

"It's not!" Nush puffed, fishing her phone out of her pocket to show Nani-Ji a FaceSpace article. A pop-up appeared. Nush groaned, pressed "AGREE" and carried on scrolling.

EIGHT THINGS THEY ARE NOT TELLING YOU ABOUT TREES

They block out the sunlight

They fall over in storms and damage cars

Their roots cause damage to houses and offices

Their sharp branches can pierce skin

Their leaves block drains and pipes

They steal compounds from the air

They steal nutrients from the soil

They are not edible

Roben and 291 others   55 comments

Like   Comment   Share

Nani-Ji glanced over, then waved her hand in the air. "Pah, nonsense, my little beta."

"It's not nonsense!" Nush protested. "And the vote is happening this Sunday! Please vote for the Cyber Oak!" Nush's cheeks reddened. "Every vote counts. Trees are totally not OK any more, like ... like ... smoking, and sexism, and—

"Nush, leave Nani-Ji alone – it's her birthday!" Mum cut in. There was a second's silence, and Tumble, who had been fiddling around with a small speaker, seized the moment. All this talk of trees was distracting him from his favourite subject – himself.

"Hey, guys. I've planned a dance for Nani-Ji's big birthday! I've been practising all week. It's to the tune of 'Winner'!" Tumble loved the song "Winner" from "Show Off", a dancing pets competition on TV. He cleared an imaginary dance floor and yelled, "Play 'Winner' by MC Dog."

The whole family went silent as the music played.

Yo yo yo, I'm the dog MC.
My ears are soft and my tail is wa-gg-ly.
I eat biscuits for breakfast.
I serve rhymes for my dinner.
Other dogs sniff my bum
'Cos they know I'm a winner.

Tumble jerked out of time with the beat of the song. All his moves were wrong.

"Come on, Tumble – like this!" Asha began to dance a mix of body-popping and bhangra that she'd learned in classes after school. It was too fast for Tumble. He tripped over his feet and fell flat on his tummy, paused for a moment, then pushed his bum in the air.

"Style it out, Tumble, style it out," he said quietly to himself and wiggled his bum at Nush.

"Such old tech," Nush muttered under her breath.

"Ignore her; I've got an idea," said Asha. "All we need is an algorithm." She pulled out her tablet, opened the terminal and started typing lines of code. Her fingers flew over the keyboard.

"Nearly done. Dancing is much easier if you break it down and move one step at a time." She tapped "RUN" to update Tumble's codebase. "OK. Chalo!"

You think your farts smell bad?
Well, dog farts hurt your eyes.

This time Tumble and Asha moved as
one to the beat. Tumble's screen was a
blur of emojis as they sang along.

They make the world go fuzzy
Like you've been hypnotized.

Tumble clawed at his eyes. Everyone
was laughing and clapping.

So when it comes to voting,
There's only one choice.
Vote for MC Dog, y'all.
I need to hear your voice!
Let's give a big love shout-out

To the special Nani-Ji,
The oldest person here today.
Hooray – you're seventy!

Tumble did a final shimmy, and
Asha ended on a freeze, holding a hand to her ear.
Someone started chanting, "MC DOG! MC DOG!"
and soon everyone joined in.

"TUMBLE! TUMBLE!" said Tumble, trying to
change the chant. No one listened.

As everyone settled down, Asha decided to sneak
off and investigate the hidden camera again. But as
soon as she started easing herself away, she felt a
drop of rain splash on her nose, and then another.
Typical. Everyone started checking their watches,
gathering their things and saying goodbye. Mum
would kill Asha if she disappeared now. She'd have
to come back and look later.

At the park gates, a poster caught Asha's eye. It
was bright pink and attached to the railings.

"Cool, the vote is only 48 hours away!"

DO YOU WANT TO
MAKE YOUR CITY GREENER, CLEANER AND BETTER?

THIS IS YOUR CHANCE!

Vote for Wembley Park to be the world's FIRST site for the Cyber Oak™, the revolutionary digital tree.

VOTE

✓

YES

to upgrading old-fashioned natural trees.

VOTE

✓

YES

for the trees of the future.

Voting OPENS at 15:00 Sunday 8 August.
Go to www.cyberoak.life to join the future.

SCAN ME

Nush was standing right next to Asha and by the smell of her breath, had been eating cheese and onion crisps. Nush took out her phone and started writing a FaceSpace post.

"I'm sharing with everyone."

Asha wasn't really listening. She'd noticed something on the sign. It was a logo shaped like a heart. The exact same shape she had seen engraved on the camera in the tree. There was something strangely familiar about it. Asha quickly scanned the little heart with her watch, and pressed "search".

A result popped up instantly: *The trademark Shelly*

Heart is registered to Shelly Inc, One Love Road, Loop City, London.

Asha's heart stopped dead. She re-read the sign three times just to make sure she hadn't made a mistake.

Shelly Inc? Again?

"Asha, Nush, chalo!" called Mum, who was already halfway up the street and had her hands on her hips. "No standing about in the rain – you'll catch a cold. Home time!"

"Coming!" yelled Asha, taking a quick picture of the sign. Asha had crossed paths with Shelly before and she knew one thing – if Shelly Belly was involved, it was bad.

Very, very bad.

Chapter 2

-... . .-- .- .-. . / --- ..-. / ..-. .- -.- . / -. .
.-- ... .-.-.-

19:02

"What a picnic!" said Dad, dumping a big box of empty dishes and cutlery by the sink. Asha was next in, carrying leftovers in old ice cream tubs, with Mum close behind, holding three bags of food in each hand and a rolled-up rug wedged under her arm.

"Breaking news. Trees in Toronto, Canada, have fallen over in a storm, damaging nearby cars. Angry locals have gathered nearby, chanting, 'Trees smell like mouldy cheese.' Would you like to hear more?" Putie, the smart speaker, glowed blue.

"No. Putie, please stop," Mum said, sitting down at the table. Asha wondered if adults in Canada would really shout at trees. Adults did ridiculous things all the time, and Dad always shouted at the referee when the football was on TV, so maybe it was true. Putie didn't say where she got her news, which made it harder to check.

Dad was still babbling about the party. "Lovely to see all the cousins growing up so fast," he said. Asha zoned out as she hunted through the ice cream tubs, lifting the corner of each lid and peering in. "And even Aunt Meera said my jalebi were 'quite tasty'," Dad continued, to no one in particular. "That's high praise – you know how she wrinkles her nose at everything."

Bingo! Asha had found the pakoras.

"Get a plate!" said Mum. Asha paused, her mouth wide open, a pakora poised in front of her teeth. Why were all mums obsessed with plates? It's not like they did anything. She stuffed the whole thing in her mouth before Mum could stop her, crumbs falling down her front.

"Now, Asha, Nush – you both promised me you'd do your homework tonight," said Mum.

"But it's the holidays," said Nush, slumping into a chair and scrolling through her phone. "We're not going back to school for ages."

"Still," said Mum, "you shouldn't leave it to the last minute."

Putie piped up again. "Breaking News. Shelly Belly, the world's youngest CEO, reveals her latest plans for the eagerly debated Cyber Oak."

Asha's ears pricked up. She stopped chewing and moved a little closer to the speaker.

"Dubbed the 'tree of the future', the Cyber Oak might have its first test site at Wembley Park. The decision rests on the shoulders of local residents,

who are being encouraged to vote 'yes' to Shelly's latest invention this Sunday. The vote takes place in just forty-four hours and—"

"Putie, I said STOP!" said Mum.

"But, Mum, it's about the climate," said Nush, sitting up. "Putie, continue." Asha's sister only ever seemed to get excited about two things: music and the environment.

Putie lit back up. "Created by Shelly Inc, the Cyber Oak is claimed to clear the air of methane. Speaking earlier today, Shelly Belly made a plea to all the residents of Wembley to vote 'yes'."

Shelly Belly's silky voice filled the kitchen. "The climate is real. It's big and it's airy. We all deserve the best climate ever. That's why I'm counting on you, Wembley, to stand behind the Cyber Oak. Your role is critical. After we win Wembley, we can roll the Oaks out across London and beyond! Let's show the world how to use technology for good. Do the right thing. Vote 'yes' to the Cyber Oak."

Nush nodded keenly.

"And for any local activists out there, applications are now open for our flash internship. We're offering 48 hours at Shelly HQ, London, where you'll learn how to be a climate influencer with the very special, one and only..." Shelly paused dramatically, "DJ Bestlyfe."

"OMG NO WAY!" Nush leapt up and pulled her phone out of her pocket. DJ Bestlyfe was the reason Nush had started making music, and she'd been a mega fan for years. "NOWAYNOWAY! This is so cool!" said Nush. "I'm applying right now," she gushed, tapping away at her screen.

Asha's stomach flipped. "But … you don't know anything about Shelly. Maybe she's not as great as everyone thinks. And why is she suddenly so interested in the climate? Who knows if the Cyber Oak can really reverse climate change?" The words came out a little faster and louder than Asha had intended.

"What are you talking about?!" flared Nush, staring at her sister. "You don't know anything about Shelly Belly! The only thing you know about is boring computers."

In fact, Asha knew more about Shelly Belly than Nush could ever imagine.

On Asha's last spy mission, Shelly had tried to destroy the world's Internet, and had gone head-to-head with Asha in a deadly boat fight. But Asha couldn't tell Nush a single thing about being a spy. She was sworn to secrecy.

"I'll support anything that's good for our planet. But I do love our little park and I can't imagine it without real trees!" said Mum, tearing Asha away from her thoughts.

"The most important thing is that we all have the right to vote. It's a privilege to have a say in how our local parks are run," Dad chipped in.

"I'm just saying, perhaps there's more to the Cyber Oak than you think." Asha looked at her dad, frustrated.

"Whatever you say, you can't deny that Shelly is very successful. She must have studied very hard at school!" Dad drew his arm around Asha's shoulder and gave her a squeeze.

"Actually, Dad," said Asha, "Shelly left school when she was sixteen to start her own business..." Then she changed her mind mid-sentence. "But maybe you're right. I should go upstairs immediately and study." Mum and Dad looked at her in stunned silence. Asha hopped off the counter and ran out of the kitchen.

As she raced up the stairs with Tumble, she heard her sister whoop.

"I got in!" yelled Nush. "I start tomorrow!"

Chapter 3

.- .-.. .-- .- -.-- ... / .-. . .- -.. / - .... . /
... -- .- .-.. .-.. / .--. .-. .. -. - .-.-.-

20:38

Asha shut her bedroom door. "Drone, keep watch," she said.

Keeping secrets from her family was hard. On top of a snooping sister and parents who wanted to know every single detail of her life, Asha had aunties, uncles and cousins coming out of her ears. In fact, Asha's grandma – Nani-Ji – ran what everyone jokingly called "the KBC" – the Kenton Broadcasting Cooperation. Whenever any news reached Nani-Ji, within minutes the extended family, and all their neighbours and friends in the Kenton and Wembley area, would know about it. If you wanted to find anything out, you just needed to ask the KBC.

"Set perimeter. Load heat maps. Turn noise sensitivity to high," Drone replied, loading the GuardDog code Asha had written. "Floorboard sensors activated. Initializing the SNORT."

Like all landings in all houses everywhere, there was a squeaky floorboard at the top of the stairs. And like all self-respecting kids, both Asha and Nush knew exactly where it was, and how to sidestep it. They used to get up to all sorts of mischief together when their parents thought they were asleep: midnight feasts, duvet-den-making and one time sneaking out before dawn to hide under a bush and watch the fox cubs in the garden come out to play.

But at some point Nush had grown out of sneaking out with Asha, and grown into sneaking up on her. She burst into Asha's room without knocking all the time. So Asha had installed a secret sensor system on the floorboards just outside her door, and programmed it to make Tumble snort when anyone was there. If Nush came too close,

Asha would know about it.

This was especially important now that Asha was a spy.

Well, at least, she was almost a spy.

Asha had recently joined the Children's Spy Agency and completed her first mission. But she had broken a few rules along the way, and the CSA had placed her on "probation", which meant she hadn't been fully accepted into the Agency. Not yet, anyway. This could be her chance.

"The Cyber Oak vote is on Sunday. That's in 48 hours," Asha said, pacing up and down.

"Incorrect. The voting opens at 3 p.m., which is less than 42 hours from now," Drone beeped.

"That's not much time at all."

Shelly was up to something – Asha could feel it in her bones. She just needed to prove it. In only two days' time, it could be the end for all the trees in Wembley Park. They might be chopped down. Trees that had been there for hundreds of years. What would happen then? Investigating the Cyber Oak could be just the mission Asha needed to become an access-all-areas, fully-fledged spy.

Asha paced even faster. She took out her phone to look at the picture she'd taken in the park. It had a web address on it. Asha typed in the URL and was led to a bright green Cyber Oak website. There was a live feed of FaceSpace posts using the hashtag #CyberOak. She scrolled past loads of messages saying "Vote yes!", "So hype!" and "Trees are so bad!"

Further down, Asha found two big buttons – "Register to Vote!" and "How to Vote Yes!"

Neither of those were right, so she clicked on the "Contact Us" link at the bottom of the page.

A new page loaded, with a big green tick.

"No!" Asha muttered to herself. She'd been tricked into signing up for a mailing list.

"Did you see that?" Asha turned to Drone.

"Yes, that was strange. I worry there might be an error in the code."

"Yeah, maybe," Asha mumbled, biting her lip. Asha was really proud of Drone's computing power, which was gigantic, especially for such a small robot. Drone could search the web at lightning speed, and process information in nanoseconds. Plus, Drone was fiercely loyal. Asha tried to focus on this, and not on the fact that she had to put up with Drone's worrying.

"Have you found anything else on the Cyber Oak yet?" Asha asked.

"Initial search complete. I have analysed 523 posts on FaceSpace," Drone replied. "97 per cent of posts are in support of the Cyber Oak. However, there are rumours on the Dark Web that the science is fake," she continued.

FaceSpace

InsiderJoe
@InsiderJoe

@InsiderJoe here. Security by day, whistle-blower by night. Two months ago, got a job on this Shelly Inc project ... got paid loads ... the great Shelly herself was there sometimes – she licked her weird monkey-panda pet thing on the nose when she thought no one was looking. Anyway ... was asked to shred reports on Cyber Oak Beta ... read them. Those trees are BAD news. Something shady going on. Big company lying to us ... again.
Follow **@InsiderJoe** for more info.

"I tried to follow @InsiderJoe, but their account has been suspended," Drone beeped. "But I did locate a picture of the Cyber Oak. The metadata tag is 'Orkney'."

"Orkney?" asked Asha, confused. "What's Orkney?"

"Duh! Haven't you seen 'The Orkney Factor'?" Tumble chipped in. "Kids get dropped on this island and have to find their own food for a month. They can't even bring their phones. It's set in, ummm, mmmm..." Tumble's geography wasn't as good as his knowledge of reality TV.

"The Orkney Islands are off the north coast of Scotland," Drone beeped. "I also found a blueprint of the Cyber Oak." Drone projected a drawing of the tree onto the far wall.

"Oooh, selfie sticks that double up as branches!" exclaimed Tumble. "That's GENIUS! And look, Asha, it can create FaceSpace filters too! Game-changing!"

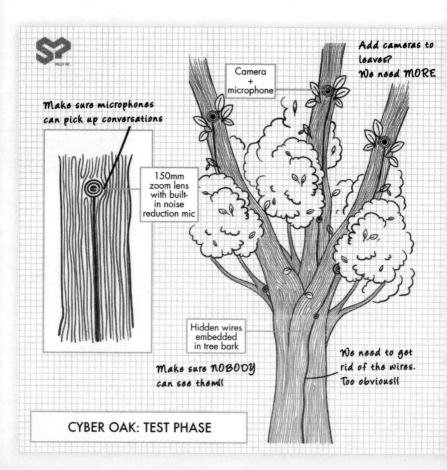

Asha's mind was thundering like a washing machine full of trainers. There was no explanation for how the trees actually cleaned the air. The Cyber Oak website had tricked her, and then there was Insider Joe's post. The more she thought about it, the more suspicious it seemed.

There was only one thing to do next.

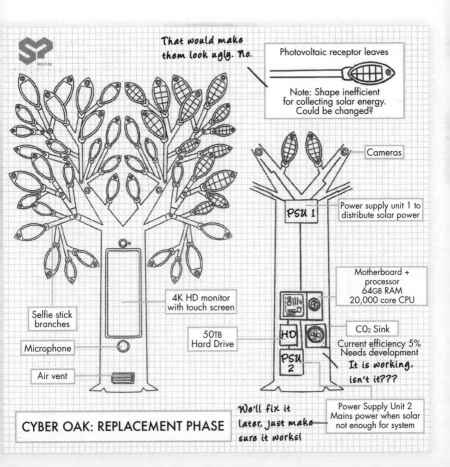

CYBER OAK: REPLACEMENT PHASE

Asha fired up her laptop and held down three keys: the letters C, S and A. Blue letters typed into view.

Asha pulled a notebook out from her desk drawer. Hidden inside was a tablet. She held it up to her ear.

"You look just like Nani-Ji on a video call!" Tumble mimed Asha talking to her grandma. "Yes, Nani-Ji, it's me. No, you're on video. All I can see is your ear." He raised his voice. "VIDEO call, Nani-Ji. Yes, it is very clever!" Tumble fell over laughing. He was the only thing Asha knew – person, robot or otherwise – that actually rolled on the floor laughing.

"Stop!" said Asha, stifling her giggles. As the tablet finished

scanning her ear, her watch buzzed on her wrist. It was running a test – gathering information about her heart rate, blood pressure and temperature. This was all part of Asha's unique biometric "fingerprint".

The Children's Spy Agency's security was extreme.

A beep sounded. Asha loved this bit.

There was a low hum in the room and then everything went dark.

Heart rate:	72bpm	✓
Temperature:	37.5°C	✓
Step count:	11,754	✓
Daily Fart count:	23*	✓

*Recommendation: eat smaller meals more frequently, with fewer beans.

Verifying...

IDENTITY VERIFIED

INITIALIZING CSA MODE
ACTIVATE CSA MODE

| MY MISSIONS | MY TRAINING | MY INTEL |

CSA GUIDE TO MIND CONTROL: BAD BUTTONS

Agents, beware of Bad Buttons

Some apps and websites use confusing or manipulative
pictures, buttons and words to control people.

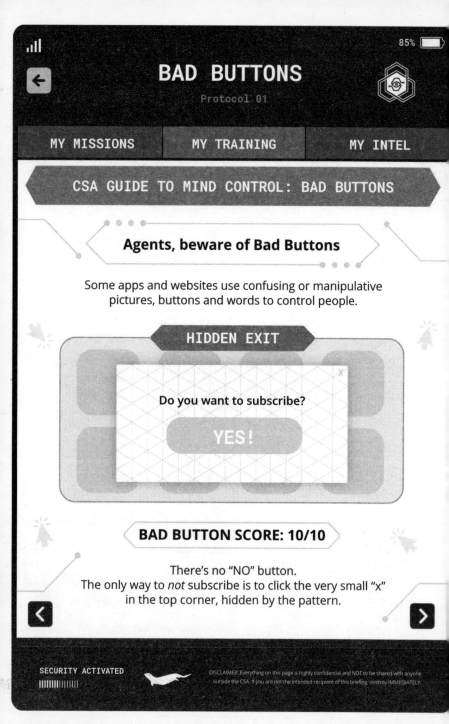

HIDDEN EXIT

x

Do you want to subscribe?

YES!

BAD BUTTON SCORE: 10/10

There's no "NO" button.
The only way to *not* subscribe is to click the very small "x"
in the top corner, hidden by the pattern.

‹   ›

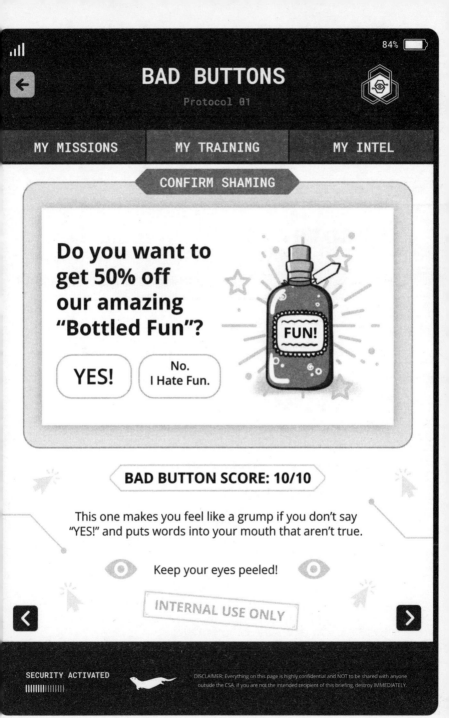

Chapter 4

..- ... . / --. .- -.. --. . - ... / .-. . ... .--.
--- -. ... .. -... .-.. -.-- .-.-.-

21:09

Asha's bedside lamp turned green, bathing the whole room in a spooky glow.

The walls and curtains shimmered with holographs, and lines of code flickered across them as they were written and edited in real time. There were rolling news feeds, live chats and the latest reports from agents around the world. Even the soles of Asha's trainers lit up with a soft blue-green light. They were on standby for Flashbang Mode. Asha just needed to click the heels together twice.

Asha's bedroom had transformed into a

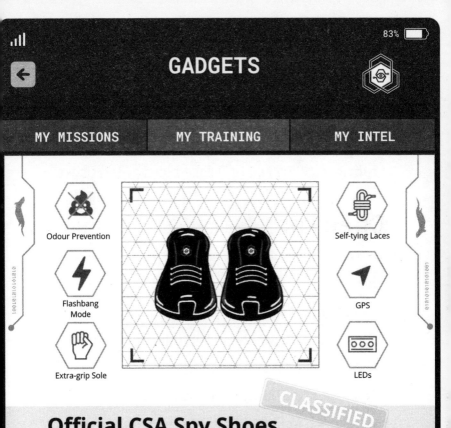
Odour Prevention

Self-tying Laces

Flashbang Mode

GPS

Extra-grip Sole

LEDs

CLASSIFIED

Official CSA Spy Shoes

The CSA Spy Shoes should be worn on all official missions. With slime spray to assist in sticky situations, extra strong lace-rope for emergency zip lines, hidden cameras, GPS and walking pattern analysis biometrics to enable extra features, this amazing footwear is ideal for covert spy operations.

Specs:

TOP SECRET

- </> CAUTION! Slime button
- </> Hidden LED bulbs
- </> Sensors to activate LEDs
- </> Soggy feet prevention + extra-strong odour eaters

- </> Extra-grip sole
- </> Built in GPS
- </> Flashbang Mode
- </> Glitterbang Mode
- </> Superglue Mode

>

personal bunker for the Children's Spy Agency – a global network of spy kids who were dedicated to fighting injustice and uncovering the truth.

The CSA was organized by a super-smart Artificial Intelligence (AI) called Hedy. Hedy knew everything and had access to the coolest gadgets Asha had ever seen. And Hedy also decided who passed probation to become a proper spy, and when.

"Yes! Your shoes! Goo time!" Tumble darted across the room and hit a bright green button on Asha's left heel. A stream of green goo sprayed right over his head, landing with a splat behind him. Asha had forgotten about the goo function. She turned to look at the mess.

"WARNING! WARNING!" Drone beeped furiously, hovering close to the carpet. "Goo may cause slips, trips and carpet stains."

A robot

pipe unfolded underneath Drone, as her screen continued to flash. "Goo-suction in progress. Updating health and safety log."

"Well, that was fun." Tumble gave Asha his cutest "I'm a little toy" look. "Now let's try Glitter-bang!" he continued, his finger poised over another button on Asha's right heel.

"NO!" Asha and Drone yelled at once. Before Tumble had a chance to hit the button, a pool of light beamed into the centre of the room, and a giant holographic dog in sunglasses appeared on the carpet, smiling.

Tumble squealed. "OH MY BATTERIES! MC DOG IS IN THE HOUSE!" He picked up his tiny phone and clicked "record".

"You will not believe this, friendos! We're at Tumble HQ doing some top-secret stuff, and then – BAM! – we're joined by the one, the only—"

Asha snatched his phone and turned it off. Tumble was obsessed with filming every single moment of his life. Even though Asha had changed his phone settings so he couldn't upload anything to the Internet, he recorded everything as if it was live, and edited it at the end of each day for Asha to check.

"Tumble, this is secret. That means no vlogging. And it's not MC Dog. It's just Hedy – remember?" Asha pinched the top of her nose in exasperation, just like she'd seen Nani-Ji do, and turned back towards Hedy.

The hologram crackled, broke up and reformed as a pillow with a smiley face. "Greetings, Agent Asha."

"Greetings," said Asha, standing up straight. "How are you, Captain Hedy?"

"I am not a captain. I cannot sail a boat. I am a hologram." Hedy paused. "Small talk complete."

"Er, OK, cool." Asha was silent for a second. "I'm reporting a new mystery about Shelly Belly and the Cyber Oak. Do you know anything about it?"

"Affirmative. We have been gathering intelligence on the Cyber Oak for the last 76 days," said Hedy, who always seemed to be a hundred steps ahead.

"It was born inside ShellyPlex, which is a complex, secretive arm of Shelly Inc. Our agents have been at work in Shelly's test site in Orkney, Scotland, running tests. They have reported serious malfunctions and a site closure. 183 wild animals have since been lost in the surrounding area."

Asha's heart skipped a beat as she wondered which animals might have been affected.

"Shelly has tried to bury the results, and is running a fake news campaign to confuse people," Hedy continued. "She is set to launch the Cyber Oak all over the world if she wins the Wembley vote." Hedy morphed into a large tree.

?

Don't believe everything you see or hear.
Remember to apply the CSA motto at all times:

THINK FOR YOURSELF. QUESTION EVERYTHING.

¿

Scientists prove eating pencils makes you smarter!

Advertisement Feature

Ashley Hastings reports for Wolf News

In a recent study, scientists discovered a strong correlation between eating pencils and high academic performance. In a survey of 10 people with one or more university degrees, as many as 60 per cent of university graduates answered "yes" to having chewed, sucked or eaten a pen, pencil or brush in the past 30 years.

Nobel prizewinner Miriam Okoye about to eat a delicious Bob's pencil

This looks fishy... Let's look closer.

MY MISSIONS	MY TRAINING	MY INTEL

CSA ANALYSIS

1 ASSESS DATA

(1) Only 10 people with degrees were interviewed. (2) We do not know what subject the degrees were in, what grade they got or which university they got them from. (3) All they did was put a pen, pencil or brush in their mouth at some point in their life – they could have been babies at the time! (4) Only 6 out of the 10 people (just over half) said "yes".

2 CHECK THE WRITER

Ashley Hastings
Marketing Intern
Bob's Pencil Co.

Beware: Sometimes companies pretend their adverts are "news"
TIP: Check for the word "advertisement feature"

3 CHECK THE SOURCES

Miriam Okoye
@M-Okoye

January 12 5.42 PM

For the last time, I don't eat pencils! I was just thinking in that picture! Do I really need to tell you why you shouldn't eat pencils?

"So what? Aren't trees a bit..." Tumble paused, thoughtfully. "Old and musty?"

"Incorrect, little toy." Hedy turned to Tumble. "Humans need trees to capture carbon dioxide and release oxygen into the air. It helps humans to breathe and protects the Earth from the heat of the sun."

"So the Cyber Oak is bad for the planet! I knew it!" Asha said, triumphantly. "But since when does Shelly care about trees? I thought all she cared about was making money?" Asha asked Hedy.

"We have reason to believe that Shelly will use the Cyber Oak to increase her fortune. She wants people to shop in parks and to steal their private data at the same time."

Asha groaned. It all made sense now.

"Shelly has released fake news about 'natural trees'." Hedy paused. "But we do not know how the stories are spreading so fast."

"I can figure that out, Hedy, if you'll let me! I can investigate," Asha replied proudly.

Hedy turned into a timer for 34 long seconds.

Coding Skills ✓
Bravery ✓

CONSENT GRANTED

"Consent granted. You have been officially assigned to Operation Cyber Chop. Your mission is to find out what technology Shelly is using to spread the fake news."

"Thank you, Hedy." Asha felt her cheeks turn pink. "I will do whatever it takes."

"Sending the CSA report on the Cyber Oak to you now. Asha, there is much more at stake than ever before. If the residents of Wembley vote 'yes' to the Cyber Oak, Shelly will start replacing all the natural trees on our planet. Without trees, our global ecosystem will collapse. This could herald the end of humanity."

Asha took a deep breath. Hedy shape-shifted again, appearing now as a pile of Asha's dirty socks.

"The CSA will be on standby. I have organized the van for your use. Remember, Asha, you are on probation. Do not be reckless. Follow the CSA protocols. We are counting on you."

With that, Hedy flickered and disappeared.

Asha felt a tingle in her toes. She loved this part of an investigation – the very start. In her mind's eye, she started mapping out information, breaking down the big problem into smaller parts, and trying to find links. The first and best question was always the same: *why?*

Asha wrote furiously in her notebook and then inspected her own plan. "Online research will only get us so far. We need to get inside."

She fiddled with her ear as she thought through her options. "We'll get caught if we walk straight into Shelly's office."

Operation Cyber Chop

MISSION:
How is Shelly spreading fake news so fast and WHY?????

GOAL: save the treeeeeees!

THE PLAN:
1. Desktop research.
2. Break into Shelly's London HQ and look for intelligence. If we can't find anything, go to test site in Orkney and see what we can find there.
3. Find out how Shelly is spreading fake news.
4. Tell everyone the truth.
5. Don't die. NO

"Nush is going tomorrow. We could watch her FaceSpace posts about it?" Tumble suggested.

"Oooh!" replied Asha. "Or we can tag along and pretend we're interns too! Nush won't mind."

"That would breach CSA Protocol 7," warned Drone. "You cannot tell anybody about the CSA. That includes siblings."

<Case files>   <Suspect files>   <Fake news>   <Top secret>   <Missions>

CASE BRIEFING: OPERATION CYBER CHOP

Operatives:

1

Agent Asha

CSA Agent
On probation

2

Tumble

Modified Poopless Pet
Approved

3

Drone

Modified Nannybot
Approved

Suspect:

Shelly Belly

- Tech entrepreneur
- Goal is to dominate global data and make money
- Suffers from sidonglobophobia

CSA RECORD:

Attacked the internet (see Operation Shark Bytes). The UK government did not press charges. Ongoing investigation.

SUSPECT

<Case files> <Suspect files> <Fake news> <Top secret> <Missions>

CSA BRIEFING:
OPERATION CYBER CHOP

Intelligence:

File:
JPEG photograph

Metadata Location:
N: 58.9662, W3.2965

Coordinates:
Stromness, Orkney
Islands, SCOTLAND

Read full report of test
sites **here**

Location:

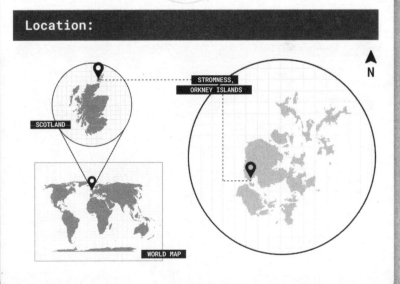

STROMNESS,
ORKNEY ISLANDS

SCOTLAND

WORLD MAP

N

"Oh, yeah." Asha's shoulders dropped. She didn't normally care about the rules, but she was desperate to pass her spy probation. She stared at her desk, which was piled high with her latest gadget ideas, a glow-in-the-dark pen and a badge her best friend Demola had given to her at school.

"Wait, I've got it!" Asha pulled her toolbox out from under her bed, grabbed a screwdriver and rummaged through nuts and bolts. Then she found it: Tumble's old phone. "I knew this would be useful for something!"

"That old thing? Really? The camera is tiny. The whole thing is tiny, even for me," said Tumble.

"That's exactly why it's perfect," said Asha,

picking up the badge from her desk and poking a small hole in it. "Drone, please could you print a sticker with 'ECO-WORRIER' written on it?" Asha asked, putting the badge to one side and turning Tumble's phone over. She unscrewed the back cover and carefully removed the circuit board, camera and microphone, rearranging the parts onto the back of the badge. The printer made a gurgling noise, before spitting out a small sticker. Asha stuck it onto the front of the badge and smoothed it over.

"Ta-da! We have a secret badge-camera!" Asha wasn't just good with computers – she could do crafty stuff too.

"Love it!" Tumble high-fived Asha.

"I'll give it to Nush, then we'll be able to see what's going on inside Shelly HQ."

Drone was about to remind Asha of her homework responsibilities when the light in her bedroom changed from green to red.

"Mood lighting. I – SNORT – love it – SNORT," said Tumble. "Oh, excuse me," he snorted.

"The warning snort!" said Asha, panicking. She swiped open her tablet and hit the

pizza emoji in the top left corner – an emergency button to cover up her spy activities. A pizza delivery website appeared on Asha's screen.

As the door opened, the room went dark for a moment, then the lights flicked on. "What are you doing?" said Nush, as she shuffled into Asha's bedroom.

"Nothing," said Asha, trying to act normal. She slipped the tablet under her notebook, and grabbed the badge.

"Why are you looking at pizzas again? And why is your lamp flashing red?" asked Nush. Tumble gave it a kick. "It's not," said Asha.

"Asha, you're being weird. Why are you being weird?"

"I'm NOT!" said Asha.

"What's that in your hand?"

"OK, you got me! It was supposed to be a surprise. I made a present for your internship at Shelly HQ," said Asha, handing Nush the badge.

Nush took it and smiled. "Worrier. That's smart. I like it. Thank you, little sis." She looked thoughtful for a moment. "I'm not worried, like 'worried' worried, but maybe I'm a bit ... I don't know. What will the other interns be like? I wonder if..."

"You'll be great," said Asha. "Like when you
DJ'd for the school party. You were brilliant. Just be
yourself." Asha gave her a big bear hug. Nush stood
a bit awkwardly, then struggled free. Asha smiled.
"Anyway, er, I need to fart so you should probably
leave now." She needed space to think.

"Gross." Nush wrinkled her nose, heading for
the door.

Chapter 5

... .--. --- - / ... --- -- . / -... --- - ... -.-.--

August 07 - 08:49

The gang were on their way to Shelly HQ in a CSA van. From the outside, you wouldn't look at it twice: it was just a big, lumbering van with some faded books in the rear window. An old coffee cup was wedged into the space between the dashboard and the windscreen, and a mean-looking librarian sat in the driving seat. The coffee cup and the librarian were both decoys. The van was self-driving, and the librarian was a hologram – no actual human had sat anywhere near the driving seat for years.

Towards the back of the van, there were shelves and shelves of books. But hidden just beyond was the official CSA surveillance zone. Large screens covered the walls, switches blinked, and LED bulbs lit the outline of a trapdoor on the floor. A couple of the screens displayed rolling news feeds and updates from the CSA network; the rest showed live video feeds from the van's cameras.

Asha focused on the news bulletin. Next to the presenter stood a young woman in an oversized green tracksuit and thick-rimmed glasses.

"Drone, who's that?" asked Asha. "Run facial recognition."

"Come on, slow coaches!" said Tumble. "That's DJ Bestlyfe! She's a legend on FaceSpace."

The sound of the news report filled the van. "...let's chat to our guest, noted record producer and musician DJ Annie Bestlyfe, who promises to fill us in on the century's most exciting invention. DJ Bestlyfe, welcome."

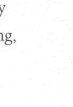

"DJ-B in the mix!" said DJ Bestlyfe. "LION! I cannot wait for the Cyber Oak to drop. It doesn't just clean the air. The Cyber Oak knows who you are. It gets you. You get me? And every time you use a Cyber Oak to buy something, it saves the climate. So cool!"

How can a tree know who you are? Asha remembered the hidden camera she'd seen in the park the day before. And wasn't that illegal?

"So we can use the trees to shop?" asked the newsreader.

"Bang on! Shop till you drop, so the planet don't stop. Trees have killed 189 people this year! They need an upgrade. Come on, Wembley, let your hearts beat for this!" DJ Bestlyfe turned and looked straight at the camera. "Drop a vote for the Cyber Oak; drop a vote for the future. LION!"

"A future we can all believe in," said the newsreader. "Let's hope they work, because Wembley is just the start – Shelly plans to roll these out all over the world. Thank you, DJ Bestlyfe."

The news report finished, and the weather jingle came on. Asha switched it off and checked the social dashboard – #CyberOak was trending, and DJ Bestlyfe was gaining thousands of followers on FaceSpace every second. Zooming in on the feed, Asha frowned. DJ-B's last update had been posted 2 minutes ago and it already had 76 million reposts.

FaceSpace

@djbestlyfe shared a post ...

Go do your thing, Wemmy peeps. Cyber Oak YES!

#CyberOak
#NoBarkAllByte
#UpgradeEarth

"Isn't DJ Bestlyfe great?" said Tumble. "She makes all the science so easy to understand. And I just love how she says LION!"

"It's not science unless there is evidence!" said Drone, who was busy fact-checking everything.

"Yeah, well, it's not science unless it's LION," Tumble replied.

Asha zoned out. How could DJ Bestlyfe's posts have been reposted 76 million times so quickly when she only had 1.2 million followers? Even for a big influencer like her, 76 million reposts seemed extraordinary. That was more than all of the people who lived in the United Kingdom. And in 2 minutes?

The numbers didn't add up. Hedy was right, the fake news was spreading faster than was humanly possible. And if it wasn't humans spreading this, then what? Asha's thoughts branched out in all directions.

"Drone, could you run an analysis on the #CyberOak hashtag and on DJ Bestlyfe's followers?"

Drone's pixels flashed red as she crunched the data. "It appears that 80 per cent of DJ Bestlyfe's followers might be spambots."

"Bots!" Tumble squealed in delight. "Bots, Asha, bots! Stinky, farty bottoms!"

"Not a human bottom, mini-brains!" Drone exclaimed. "Bot is short for 'ro-B-O-T'. Spambots are not real people. They are computer programs that create fake accounts and spread fake news."

"Right, yep. Spambots," Asha said, winking at Tumble.

If Shelly was using spambots, they must be created by a computer somewhere. Or, more

SPAMBOTS
Protocol 02

MY MISSIONS	MY TRAINING	MY INTEL

Agents, take note. There are thousands of "people" online who are not people at all. They are fake accounts, created by spambots. Spam bots are used by trolls*, companies and governments, and by people on social media who want more "likes".

*Internet trolls. For the CSA guide to Scandinavian Trolls, read this.

BEWARE OF THE FOLLOWING SIGNS OF A BOT:

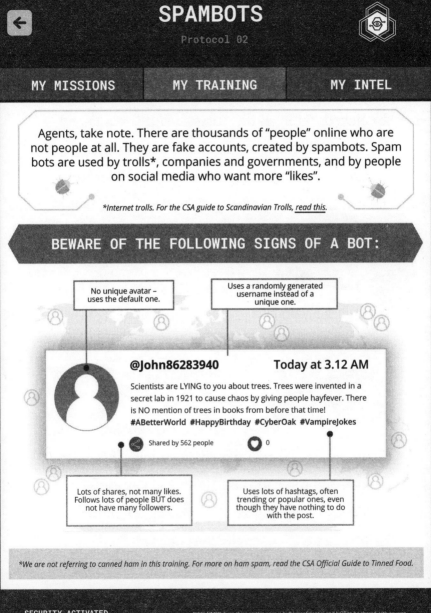

No unique avatar – uses the default one.

Uses a randomly generated username instead of a unique one.

@John86283940   Today at 3.12 AM

Scientists are LYING to you about trees. Trees were invented in a secret lab in 1921 to cause chaos by giving people hayfever. There is NO mention of trees in books from before that time!
#ABetterWorld #HappyBirthday #CyberOak #VampireJokes

Shared by 562 people   ♡ 0

Lots of shares, not many likes. Follows lots of people BUT does not have many followers.

Uses lots of hashtags, often trending or popular ones, even though they have nothing to do with the post.

*We are not referring to canned ham in this training. For more on ham spam, read the CSA Official Guide to Tinned Food.

likely, a whole load of computers. It would take a lot of computers to create 76 million fake accounts and do all that posting.

Asha remembered reading about a "server farm" in Nevada, USA. It was a building that contained hundreds of thousands of computers doing stuff all the time. Maybe Shelly was using something like that? That was a lead.

Asha started to make a note in her notebook, but the van turned sharply and she lost her grip. It was auto-parking right opposite Shelly HQ.

Asha had snuck into Shelly's London office once before, but she hadn't used the main entrance. It was huge.

"We're here!" Asha jumped up, switched on the live feed from Nush's BadgeCam and set the volume to its highest setting. The image was grainy, but it was good enough. They were looking inside a super-modern building, with rainbow-coloured bricks down two sides and glass everywhere else. From what Asha could see, the furniture looked like giant blobs of squidgy play dough, in all colours, shapes and sizes. A zip line ran down the centre of the building, through reception and out of the main exit. Robot parrots flew around inside, squawking, "Welcome to your second home!"

Nush was sat on a sofa with a small group of other nervous-looking interns. Asha had seen a few of them before at Nush's school.

"I do hope she can access fluids regularly," Drone said nervously. "Hydration is key during teenage growth spurts."

Asha rolled her eyes. "You can't worry about Nush as well." So far that morning, Drone had worried about whether Asha would need a warmer layer over her CSA bodysuit, the potential threat of an asteroid colliding with Earth in 200 years and whether Asha would be able to have her regular 2.30 p.m. poo whilst on the mission.

A man had entered the reception and was talking to the interns. He had his hair in a topknot and was holding a tablet. Asha recognized him from his hairdo instantly. It was Shelly's Chief of Staff, Ricardo Kon Carney. Yuk.

"Any questions, reach out," said the man. "My name's Ricardo, but you can call me 'bro'. We're more like a family than a workplace. Follow me!"

Asha watched as Nush followed another intern

– a tallish boy with brown hair – to the barriers. He stood still for a moment while a bright light shone on his face. The barriers slid open, and he stepped through.

"Interesting," said Asha. "Just a face scan to get in."

"Let's move, kiddos," Ricardo called. "There's a big surprise waiting for you upstairs!"

Chapter 6

- .... .. -. -.- / .- -... --- ..- - / .-- .... .- - /
-.-- --- ..- / .-. . .- -.. / --- -. .-.. .. -. . .-.-.-

10:01

Nush sat in a large room with all the other interns.
The desk, chairs and carpet were all white, and
each intern had a white screen in front of them.
Ricardo waved his arms about as he spoke.

"You have to live the dream to be on the train.
Fans are family. Content is king."

Asha was watching through the BadgeCam live
feed. From what she could see, none of the interns
had understood a word Ricardo had said. There
was a long silence.

"In other words, your job is to write FaceSpace
posts about how incredible the Cyber Oak is."

He winked. "Don't forget to hashtag #wonderfulwembley. You represent the local voice, after all!"

The screen in the van went dark, and there was lots of rustling. Nush's arm must have blocked the camera. "Stop fiddling with your ears!" Asha muttered to herself. Nush always did that when she was concentrating. The image reappeared, and the gang could see the room again.

"OK, my little clicktivists, are you with me? Good! And now – the moment you've been waiting for. The very special DJ Annie Bestlyfe is going to give us a lesson in social media, right here, right now! Hashtag #inspiring."

Asha could hear Nush gasp sharply through the microphone.

DJ Bestlyfe walked through the centre of the room and stood next to a glowing rectangular block. She wore a tracksuit and had big orange headphones draped around her neck.

"What's up, Lon-to-the-don! Fan love! I'm booming to share some of my secret sauce with you. But I don't know if you're ready..." DJ-B smiled coyly. "Are you ready?"

"Yes!" Ricardo's answer came out as a single squeak.

"I can't hear you! Crank the volume!" DJ-B

cupped a hand around her ear. "Are you ready?"

"YES! YES!" This time all the interns joined in. DJ-B's smile spread into a huge, dimpled grin. "Lion! You're ready, set, go! Here's my little secret: always follow the golden rule of the SUN!"

Asha could hear excited whispers from the crowd.

"S stands for SHORT. People have SHORT attention spans." DJ-B winked at Ricardo.

"U is for UBER-PERSONALIZED, because people deserve adverts made especially for them." DJ-B made a U shape with her arms.

"And N is for NO-THINK, because people are busy booming, and thinking kills the vibe! LION!" DJ Bestlyfe raised an arm and pointed to the sky. It was as if she was onstage at one of Shelly's global conferences, giving a talk to thousands of people. *A bit over the top for a room of thirteen interns*, thought Asha.

"Just big up voting for the Cyber Oak. Once you say it's 'eco', people will totally listen to you! LION!"

DJ-B's words were making Asha's skin crawl. She thought about the CSA's motto: Think for yourself. It was the very opposite of No-Think.

"Thank you so much, DJ-B. Very fresh advice, I think we can all agree," Ricardo said cheerfully. "Now, DJ-B has some important vlogging to do, so I'll whizz through Uber-Personalization, and then we can get started."

Through the BadgeCam, Asha saw DJ-B wave goodbye, and Ricardo point to a FaceSpace profile on a large screen. "Take Lexi here. We know her favourite colour is yellow. So, instead of showing her this picture...

...we'll show her this brighter picture..."

An intern spoke up. "But how do we know that Lexi's favourite colour is yellow?"

"Brilliant question." Ricardo grinned and pressed his hands together. His teeth were small and bright white. "FaceSpace is tracking everyone, every second! We see every single message Lexi posts, we read all of her emails and we track where she goes with her phone. Best of all, we know her entire shopping history."

Ricardo licked his lips before continuing. "So we know Lexi loves yellow because 79 per cent of the stationery she bought last year was yellow! We know the word she uses most in her emails is 'YAY!' and from her cat food orders, we can guess she has a cat. So, we'll actually show Lexi a picture like this, which means she's 70 per cent more likely to agree with us..."

Everyone murmured in amazement, but Asha could hear Nush muttering under her breath.

"Excuse me," Nush said quietly. "But is it, like, legal, to use people's private data like that?"

"Great question. I love it!" said Ricardo. "Of course we take privacy very seriously here at Shelly Inc. That's why we always get permission from our users. It's in clause 796 of our standard terms and conditions, which everyone who uses FaceSpace agrees to."

"But no one really reads those," Nush replied.

Ricardo walked towards Nush. "It sounds like someone would like to run this session herself! Would you like to take over?" Ricardo smiled his biggest smile yet while fixing

Nush with a cold stare. Nush said nothing.

"Right, I think that's enough waffle from me – you'll find instructions on your screens." Ricardo tapped a finger to his ear-mic, muttered something and moved out of sight of the BadgeCam.

The van filled with the sound of a keyboard rattling. Nush was speeding through the task. She'd written two FaceSpace posts already, starting with the climate crisis. Suddenly an ominous shadow fell across Nush's laptop. Nush sat back.

"Anushka Joshi?" said a man's voice. "Come with me, please. Bring your bag."

"What?" said Nush.

FaceSpace

@nushythefish shared a post

75% of all climate change is caused by only around 100 companies. Billionaires are one of the worst causes. #bethechange #voteYES! #wonderfulwembley #CyberOak

@nushythefish shared a post

A rise in global temperature of just a few degrees will seriously disrupt global food production and raise sea levels making many areas people live uninhabitable. #bethechange #voteYES! #wonderfulwembley #CyberOak

"Oh, don't worry," said Ricardo, looking up at her. "Probably just an admin error. See you in a mo-mo!"

"Quickly, Anushka," said the man's voice.

Nush grabbed her bag and hugged it to her chest. The BadgeCam went black, and Asha heard muffled footsteps. Through the rustling, Asha could make out Nush's voice. "Yeah, I know... I'm coming... No, I don't need any help!" Asha heard a door open and close, and then the BadgeCam picture cleared. Nush was in a much smaller room, with a bronze statue of Amanda, Shelly's special half-monkey, half-panda pet, in the corner. The man was standing over Nush.

Asha's stomach lurched.

"Who are you?" said the man.

"What?"

"Is Anushka your real name?"

"Yes, of course it is. I gave you my ID already."

"Why are you violating the terms and conditions of entry?"

"I haven't—"

"Filming without prior consent is strictly prohibited."

"Filming? I'm not filming!"

In the van, a loud siren wailed from the dashboard, and a series of bright red lights flashed. "This is bad," said Asha, as one of the screens glowed with an alert: VIDEO LINK TRACKED.

"Who do you work for?" the man continued. He had a waxy, bearded face and extremely bright eyes. He towered over Nush, glaring at the badge. To Asha, watching through the camera, it felt as though he was staring directly at her.

Asha leapt back from the screen. "Cut the video link!" she yelled. The screen went dark. "They're onto us! We have to get Nush out of there." Asha stuffed Tumble into her backpack, threw open the doors and jumped to the ground.

"CHALO!"

Chapter 7

-.. --- -. .-..-. - / - .-. ..- ... - / - .-. . . ... / -
.... .- - / ... . .-.. .-.. / - .... .. -. --. ... .-.-.-

10:56

"Be careful!" Drone called, as Asha sprinted to
the enormous glass doors. They slid open in front
of her.

A red parrot with a Shelly Inc logo on it zoomed
over. As it drew closer, Asha took in its steel panels
and plastic eyes.

"Welcome to Shelly Inc. How may I help you
today?" it said.

"Oh, hi, I'm late for my internship," Asha
panted.

"I will book you in. Take a seat," said the
parrot, as it whirred off across the lobby.

"Sorry, no time!" said Asha. She was already at the barriers. She opened a picture of Nush on her watch and held it up to the camera. She'd learned this trick at the CSA training on facial recognition – lots of security gates can't tell the difference between a real person and a picture of a person! But Asha had never actually tried it herself. She held her breath.

"**Identity verified. Welcome back, Anushka,**" a voice said. "**Find Project Cyber Oak on the third floor. Have a profitable day.**"

It worked! Asha raced through the barriers, headed straight for the lifts and hit "up". A screen above the doors showed the lift moving from floor to floor: 19 … 18 … 17 … 16 … 16... It had stopped moving. Asha could feel sweat in the palm of her hands. What if someone noticed her?

"Guys, this way!" Asha headed for the nearest fire escape, trying to stay close to the wall. Drone flew ahead, and scanned the area.

"Asha, this door is locked. You need a security card to enter," Drone beeped. "And you really should keep the stairs clear in case of an actual fire. It's a health and safety risk."

"Risk, shmisk," Asha said, whipping her CSA Copycat Card from her pocket and swiping it across the handle. The door clicked. Asha dashed up three flights of stairs, two at a time, with Drone buzzing behind.

The third floor looked like an empty kids' playground. There was grass all over the floor, the walls were climbable and there were swings dotted around, but there were no humans in sight. Tumble jumped down from Asha's backpack, and licked the grassy ground.

"It's plastic," he exclaimed excitedly.

"Everything's plastic," Asha replied, moving past a few plastic animals towards a huge tree. Instead of bark, it had a holographic skin that flowed with adverts.

"OMG, the Cyber Oak!" screeched Tumble.

As they approached, the adverts dissolved, and a new message appeared.

Loading personalized experience. FaceSpace data unavailable. Scanning...

"Good afternoon," said the tree. "Based on your height and brown hair, you must be a bear cub. Would you like to buy fresh salmon or tinned?"

"What?" said Asha.

"Based on your high-performance trainers, we think you're a professional basketball player. Would you like a protein shake?"

"This must be some kind of beta version," Asha mumbled. She scanned the room, trying to ignore the tingly feeling in her body.

Tumble extended his selfie stick and brushed down his ears. "Tumblers, tune in for my WORLD EXCLUSIVE vlog of the Cyber Oak. Here it is, peeps!" Tumble spun the camera around the room. "We've already seen some crazy cool things at Shelly HQ and now a demo of the tree itself." Tumble focused back on the robotic tree. "Hit me, Tree-face."

The tree's holographic screen displayed a huge thumbs up.

Asha decided to take a very quick look at the Cyber Oak, seeing as it was right there. Along the bottom of the screen, she noticed a settings cog and pressed it. Perhaps she could find out how it worked? But she'd probably have to break through multiple security levels first.

Asha cracked her knuckles and got ready to put her coding skills to use. A username and password screen popped up. She studied the screen for clues. Hacking into computers was usually half coding, half detective work.

There! To the bottom of the pop-up, in tiny writing, was a link: REPORT LOG.

Asha pressed it and a new screen appeared with folders in a neat column down the right-hand side. There was no password protection at all!

"What a rookie error – no security on a prototype!" Asha said to herself as she looked through the folders. She spotted a folder named "Plans" and opened it. Hundreds of files appeared. Asha scanned over them. There were images of technical drawings, maps and sea charts.

"Snooze! This tree is way boring," Tumble whispered to the camera. He was making his way around the base of the tree, taking pictures. "No banter. Just boring old maps of... Is that Scotland? Wasn't that the location for 'The Great Scottish Haggis Hero'? Let me know in the comments."

Asha narrowed her eyes, trying to make sense of it all. She was sure there was a clue in there somewhere, but she needed to focus on finding Nush. "Tumble," she whispered. "Make sure you get all this on camera. We have to get moving."

"No problem, Stinky-feet!" he said, leaning in for a close-up.

Asha looked around. Next to the tree was a picnic bench, and beyond that Asha could see a huge zip line coming through the ceiling, down to the floors below. An employee whizzed past on it, looking stressed.

Further ahead, she noticed a row of glass-walled meeting rooms. She squinted. Ricardo and the interns were in the first room. In the next room, Asha could just about make out a bronze statue of a monkey-panda on a shelf. Bingo!

"Guys, this way." Asha crouched down, and motioned to Tumble and Drone to follow her. They were halfway there when a voice blasted out of the intercom.

"ShellyParrots, report to the third floor," Ricardo's voice boomed. "A lost child needs our help urgently!"

Asha's heart beat faster. Ricardo must have seen her. She raced for the door and burst in to find Nush sitting on a metal folding chair at a large grey table, biting her fingernails.

Nush looked up, and her mouth dropped wide open. "Asha?! What are you doing here? And what are you wearing?!" She stared at Asha's blue and green bodysuit.

"I've come to get you out of here!" blustered Asha.

"Er, hello?! I'm at work, remember! My manager

is just checking something." Nush looked aghast. "You shouldn't even be here."

"Look-no-time, but-I-maybe-hooked-you-up-with-a-secret-camera, which-is-probably-illegal-sorry, and-I-think-the-guards-found-it, and-Shelly-is-actually-really-bad, and-trust-me-we-have-to-get-out-of-here-right-now. Now-now." Asha took a short breath. "I'll explain the rest later. Come on – follow me!"

Asha grabbed Nush's arm and hurtled her out of the room – straight into a rabble of security parrots. **"How may I help you?"** they screeched in unison.

"I don't need any help, thank you!" said Asha, spinning around. "Drone, are there any exits nearby?"

"The closest one is back down the stairs," answered Drone. "16.2 metres north-west, next to the ShellyShake machine!"

Asha changed direction, but it was too late. Ricardo was further down the hallway, blocking their path to the exit.

"Get down!" Asha pulled Nush to the floor and crawled behind a bouncy castle. A flock of parrots whirred past them towards Ricardo.

"Find those girls and take them to Shelly's security team. Let me know when it's done," Ricardo snapped.

Overhead, they could see the parrots fan out to search the room. Asha started to panic. She grabbed Nush and crawled back to the Cyber Oak, trying to hide behind its thick trunk.

"Would you like to hear one of our most popular songs for 99p?" the Cyber Oak boomed unexpectedly, springing into life.

"Shh, no!" said Asha. She couldn't believe she was talking to a tree.

Loading music preferences.

"Deactivate!" Asha whispered, but it was no use. The music changed, and the familiar beat of Tumble's favourite song started up. He couldn't resist swaying to the beat.

Playing MC Dog 'Winner'.

That gave Asha an idea. "The dance! Tumble, if we..."

"No explanation needed, friend," said Tumble.

He did three roly-polies and came to a stop in front of the hovering parrots. They flinched as he flipped to his feet. The lyrics kicked in, and he began to move. Tumble was dancing much better than he had at the picnic: body-popping and wiggling his bum in perfect time with the music.

Several pairs of glowing blue eyes locked on to Tumble and started to flash, as their robot bodies started spinning.

"It's working!" said Asha. "Tumble, keep going, just be unpredictable! They haven't been programmed to recognize dance moves."

"I was BORN for this!" yelled Tumble as he shimmied from side to side.

"Do not compute. Do not compute," said the parrots in unison, their speech slurring. They started to fly around in small circles.

"Oooh yeah," said Tumble, doing a little pirouette between bum wiggles. "Get a bit of that Tumble-tush!"

"Behaviour file not found. Confusion: total," said the parrots. **"Battery level: low. Roost Mode initiated."** They fluttered to the branches of the Cyber Oak, and switched off.

"Well, that's rude," said Tumble.

"That was great, Tumble. Now, time to go!" said Asha, dancing across the room towards the zip line. Ricardo was running towards them now, hand clamped to his ear.

"Send in human backup – and run a bug report!" he screamed.

Asha had a split second to press "VAN" on her watch before she bundled Nush onto the zip line with the rest of the gang.

The room disappeared in a blur.

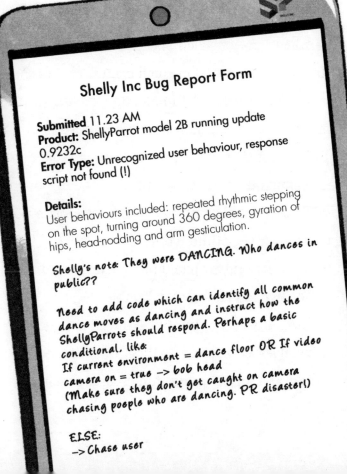

Shelly Inc Bug Report Form

Submitted 11.23 AM
Product: ShellyParrot model 2B running update 0.9232c
Error Type: Unrecognized user behaviour, response script not found (!)

Details:
User behaviours included: repeated rhythmic stepping on the spot, turning around 360 degrees, gyration of hips, head-nodding and arm gesticulation.

Shelly's note: They were DANCING. Who dances in public??

Need to add code which can identify all common dance moves as dancing and instruct how the ShellyParrots should respond. Perhaps a basic conditional, like:
If current environment = dance floor OR If video camera on = true -> bob head
(Make sure they don't get caught on camera chasing people who are dancing. PR disaster!)

ELSE:
-> Chase user

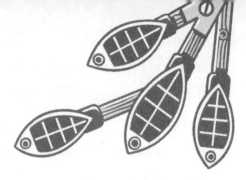

Chapter 8

.-.. --- --- -.- / ..-. --- .-. / - .... . / .-.. . - -
. .-. ... / -.-. --..-- / ... / .- -. -.. / .- .-.-.-

11:32

"You'd better start talking right now." Nush's cheeks were flushed red.

"I can explain," said Asha. "Calm down."

"You just destroyed my life! I am NOT going to calm down. I am calming up!"

"You were only writing rubbish FaceSpace posts! It was a waste of time."

"What? That was just, like, one task. And how do you even know that?"

"I saw it all on camera."

Nush stared at her.

"It's for a school project on computer science,"

continued Asha. Her upper lip felt sweaty. "We have to run surveillance on something. I picked you and gave you a camera badge. Mum said I could."

"No, she didn't. Asha, I'm not playing. Tell me what you're up to right now or I'm going back inside."

Asha couldn't let Nush do that.

"OK, fine ... I'll tell you the truth. I'm ...

on a top-secret mission investigating Shelly HQ."

Nush threw her hands in the air. "Asha, this is the last time I'm going to ask you what's really going on."

"I'm telling the truth!"

"As if! You're my little sister. I know everything

about you, and I would know if you were some kind of spy." Nush's voice wobbled. "I really, really wanted that internship. It was my chance to actually *do* something about the climate crisis."

"Look, I really am a spy! And the Cyber Oak is deadly. And natural trees aren't dangerous at all; that's just fake news!"

Nush was silent, so Asha continued. "DJ Bestlyfe seems to be in on it too. If Shelly wins the vote on Sunday, Wembley Park will be destroyed, and then even worse things will happen! I have to stop her."

Nush paused and looked around the van, her eyes narrowing as she took in all the dusty old books. "OK. Let's say for a moment that you actually are a spy. Prove it. Show me ... I don't know ... a spy gadget."

"I can't! I'm sworn to secrecy!"

"Shworn to sheecweshy," scoffed Nush. "Right, I'm out of here. Mum and Dad are going to kill you."

"No! Wait!" If Nush went back inside Shelly HQ, Asha's mission would be over. Asha took a deep breath and held out her little finger.

"You can't tell anyone, ever. Pinkie promise."
Nush thought about it for a moment, then hooked
her finger around her sister's. The Joshis never broke
a pinkie promise.

Asha reached up and held her CSA Copycat Card
against the spine of a dark navy book called *Chewy
Spaghetti Armageddon!* The bookshelf glowed into
life, and the books tipped up and back. A console
slid out from behind them, and the lights dimmed.

Nush stood stock still, speechless.

Asha waited a few moments for her sister to say something, and then flicked her on the forehead.

"Do that again and you're dead," Nush snapped at her sister. "Now, spill!"

Asha told her everything – all about the Children's Spy Agency: how she'd followed a coded message to the basement of the local library, which had turned out to be a spy bunker, how she'd stolen a boat, and all about Shelly's killer sharks.

"And now," Asha took a big breath, "Shelly's up to something worse. She tested the Cyber Oak in Orkney and it was a total disaster. It killed wildlife and caused loads of pollution. It got so bad, she had to shut the test site down. I've got the reports here." Asha pointed to her tablet. Nush looked unsure.

"Now she wants to put her Oaks in Wembley, even though they are lethal," Asha continued. "She's burying the truth, and flooding the world with fake news. And DJ Bestlyfe is making it even worse – she's spreading the lies to her gazillion followers."

"No way. DJ-B would never do that."

"Would too!"

"Would not!"

The sound of a newsreader caught Asha's attention. "Wait, Tumble – turn that up!"

"...and that's not the only important vote happening this week. With only 24 hours to go, we are all relying on London to vote 'yes' to the Cyber Oak." The report showed an aerial shot of Wembley Park, then cut to a row of shiny diggers and bulldozers, all emblazoned with the Shelly Inc logo. "Shelly has made a personal appeal to everyone who lives in Wembley to vote with their hearts. Hear more from local activist, Anushka Joshi."

Nush's face came on screen as a montage of

footage from the morning played: Nush walking into reception, Nush smiling at DJ-B's talk and Nush typing on her laptop.

A silky voice spoke as the video played. "I'm Nush, and I'm a huge eco-warrior. DJ Bestlyfe is my inspo! The Cyber Oak technology is powerful enough to reverse climate change. All my friends and family are voting 'yes', this is just what Wembley – and the world – needs!"

"Voting closes on Sunday," said the newsreader, "and it looks like Shelly is all set for victory."

Nush's mouth dropped wide open. "I never said that! That's not even my voice! She sounds nothing like me!" Nush shouted at the screen. "And ... and..." Asha knew how much Nush loved DJ-B. She streamed all of her mixes and loyally defended every single music choice. "DJ-B's been lying to all her fans," Nush said, shaking her head. She turned to her sister, eyes stinging with tears. "Asha, we have to do something."

"Er, yeah, that's what I've been trying to tell you!"

said Asha, turning to Tumble. "Could you show me your photos from Shelly HQ?"

"Totes!" Tumble said, proudly beaming his photos onto the screen. The first was of a totally ordinary-looking map. Nothing special. But as they zoomed in, they could see layers and layers of extra information.

"Look – there!" Asha had spotted a pin, right in the middle of a place called Stromness, Orkney. It had a tiny label. "Drone, could you zoom in?" A word came into view: ShellyPlex.

"Maybe that's Shelly's base," said Asha, getting excited. "The one Hedy told us about. But why have a base there?"

"The sea off the coast of Orkney is freezing," Drone replied. "Tech companies build server farms there to keep their computers cold. You remember what a server is, don't you, Asha?" Drone was too excited to wait for a reply. "A server is a computer that works with other computers. So a server farm is a group of computers, with a lot of computing power! Isn't that great!"

Tumble pretended to yawn and fall asleep.

Asha's mind felt like it was full of Lego blocks, floating around, trying to fit together. One thing was nagging at her.

"What's the latest on the #CyberOak hashtag?" she asked.

"Analysing," Drone beeped and then projected the findings on the main screen in the van. The Cyber Oaks were being endorsed by over 3 presidents, 22 universities, 200 sports stars, 800 hamster accounts and 987 million people. The numbers were going up in front of their eyes.

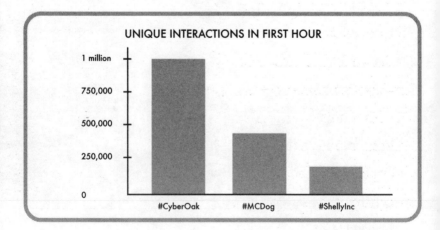

"This can't be real. It's too fast," Asha said.

"You might be right," Drone replied. "These results are irregular compared to other viral hashtags. Even news about the Queen doesn't spread this fast!" Drone said smugly.

Asha felt a tingle in her chest. She started pacing back and forth and then – BAM! It felt like all of the Lego pieces had clicked together.

"That's it! I've cracked it!" Asha leapt up and pressed the CSA button on her watch. There was a loud beep, then a huge holographic pillow appeared in the centre of the van. It was Hedy.

"Greetings, Agent Asha," Hedy boomed. "Anushka Avani Joshi detected. Protocol breach updated on mission log."

Asha's shoulders slumped, as Nush stared at Hedy in awe.

"Hedy, I am reporting in for duty on Operation Cyber Chop. I've had a breakthrough – I've figured out how Shelly is spreading the fake news so fast. She's using spambots. And I even know where they are located!" Asha said proudly.

"Excellent progress. Please continue, Agent Asha."

"Well, we found a plan of something called the ShellyPlex." Asha opened the picture and zoomed in on a series of rectangles. "It's in Orkney. See those bits underwater ... we think there are thousands of computers there. With that many computers, Shelly would be able to power millions of spambots!" Asha started to pace.

Nush looked blankly at Asha. "Spam what?!"

"Keep up, Nush – spambots!" Tumble rolled his eyes. "Computers that make fake accounts."

Drone's Cool Guide to Computer Cooling for the limited Human Brain! v2.1

Why should you put server computers under water?
Because computers love to stay cool!

Why do computers need to be cool?
Good question, human!

When electricity moves through a wire, the wire gets hot from all the energy pushing through it, just like your human hands get hot if you quickly rub them together. A computer can heat up to over 100 degrees Celsius; that's hot enough to boil an egg!

When computers get hot, it can cause two problems:
1. When circuits are hot, it changes the speed at which electricity travels through them, and stops them working properly.
2. The plastic parts may catch on fire!

Why don't you just use a fan, like humans?
Excellent thought, human!

Most computers use fans to blow cool air onto their parts, but water is even better at cooling things. Just like humans find that sitting in a pool is even better on a hot day than sitting by a fan.

"Exactly," said Asha, turning to Hedy. "So I'll hack into her computers and shut the spambots down. I can do it from here." Asha reached for her laptop.

"Negative. Shelly's firewalls are too strong for you to hack in remotely. Any attempt will alert her of our inquiry." Hedy shape-shifted into a locked door. "To shut the spambots down, you need to break into the server farm and log into the main computer."

"You know it's under water though, right?!"

"Affirmative. There are access points through the ground floor."

"Oooh, will Asha get extra mission points for this?" Tumble asked excitedly.

"I will calculate mission points at the end of the mission. The focus is on saving trees, not getting points."

"Of course," Asha replied, elbowing Tumble.

"Orkney is over 500 miles away," Hedy continued. "There are four transport options available." A table appeared on the screen.

VEHICLE	DISTANCE	TIME	CARBON EMISSIONS
Helicopter and private jet	528 miles	3 hours	388 kilogrammes CO_2
Car and ferry	696 miles	14 hours 5 minutes	173 kilogrammes CO_2
Sleeper train, local train, bus and ferry	782 miles	20 hours 29 minutes	40 kilogrammes CO_2
Bicycle and ferry	807 miles	71 hours	27 bananas each

"Oooh. Helicopter and private jet please," said Tumble. "We can be there this afternoon!"

"Yeah, private jet!" said Asha. "Just think, Tumble – mini fridge!"

"MINEH FRIDGE OOH YEAAAH!" whooped Tumble. Asha giggled.

"No way!" said Nush. "The environmental impact of us flying in a private jet is HUGE – nearly 400 kilogrammes of CO_2! That must be the weight of, what, 60 penguins?"

"Fine, let's drive," said Tumble. "The CSA can send a limo."

"The CSA is a global spy agency, not a show business company," Hedy replied. "Tickets for the Caledonian Sleeper train have been uploaded to your CSA app. You will find the CSA Spy Cabin in the centre of the train. We will arrange for special equipment and gadgets. Do not take any equipment that has not been assigned to you."

Hedy shape-shifted into a ticking clock. "There are only 24 hours left until the vote on Sunday. The mission is simple. One – break into the server farm. Two – disable the spambots. Three – stop the vote for the Cyber Oak."

Asha's stomach flipped. Stromness was further from London than she'd been before, and breaking into Shelly's server farm was not going to be easy. But Asha had broken into school once on a Sunday, and she'd also snuck into Shelly HQ. Plus, the Children's Spy Agency would be on standby.

"Got it," Asha said to Hedy, standing up tall.

"Good luck, Agent Asha. And remember, you are still on probation." Hedy changed into a puffin. "DO NOT break any more protocols."

Before Asha could protest, Hedy disappeared.

"The sleeper train is going to be ace." Nush elbowed her sister. "And once we get there, we can show DJ-B who she is messing with."

"We?" Asha shuffled on the spot. "Erm, Nush, I have to drop you home. This mission is for CSA agents only."

"What? No way! I'm totally coming!"

"Sorry, not going to happen."

"You're not even a CSA agent! You're on probation," countered Nush. Asha's eyes stung a little.

"Look, I can help you," Nush softened her tone. "It's a long way to go. Think of all the train staff – they'll be asking what a little girl like you is doing on her own. If I'm with you, that won't be a problem. I look older and I'm better at talking to adults."

Asha knew that bit was true at least.

"I'll ring Mum right now and tell her you're with me and that we're having a cousins sleepover. Millie and Rhea will totally vouch for us!" Nush said confidently.

"OK," Asha hesitated. "But you can only come as far as the ferry. I'll go to the ShellyPlex alone." Asha looked down at her feet for a second. "I can't mess up my one chance to prove myself."

Nush turned to Asha and smiled. "Shelly Belly and DJ Bestlyfe are going to wish they'd never messed with the Joshi sisters."

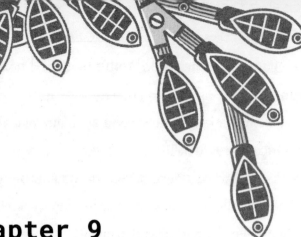

Chapter 9

... .-.. .-.. -.-- .-..-. ... / --. --- - / -.
--- - .... .. -. --. / --- -. / ..- ... .-.-.-

17:25

"What time was this exactly?" Shelly was back in her penthouse, gazing out of the window at the people in the street below. They looked like tiny ants. A voice continued to speak through her wireless earbuds. "And you didn't spot this earlier?" She listened. "Right. Just one security parrot in the lobby. Mmm-hmmm." Shelly logged into her computer. "Send me the link to the footage. And get your intelligence test early this month. I'm worried about you."

Shelly hung up, taking a deep breath, just as her life coach had told her to. She turned to Ricardo.

"Am I the only one who thinks about solutions around here?"

"Of course not, Shellz. Not at all! In fact, I've got an idea. What if—"

"Not now!" Shelly cut Ricardo off sharply.

Shelly clicked "play" and scanned the footage. The image showed a young girl with a big brown plait charging through her lobby. Shelly recognized Asha immediately.

"Oh, cute! It's that little girl again! How sweet that she's come to pay me another visit. We just can't keep her away, can we Rickybae?" Shelly's eyes were fixed on her screen. "Why is she always wearing that weird blue and green bodysuit?"

Shelly watched Asha make her way from the lift, to the stairs, all the way to Anushka. "Ah, and is that her sister? Absolutely gorgeous! Can anything beat sisterly love?"

Ricardo fidgeted with his necklace, trying to find the best time to confess. Maybe now? He cleared his throat, but Shelly silenced him with a wave of her hand. "Not yet, Face-ache! No spoilers. Ah-ha! So this is when you come to collect our little runaways."

"Well, actually, there was a malfun—"

"Is that a mouse?" Shelly interrupted, spotting Tumble. "And why have the parrots stopped flying?"

"Well, Shelly." Ricardo took a deep breath. "The parrots seemed to have a glitch ... and ... the girls got away."

Shelly's face twitched ever so slightly. She opened the ShellyParrot logs and looked for the bug. "Error 413. Unidentified behaviour," she muttered.

ERROR 413

The ShellyParrots were in the final stages of development. They were going to replace standard house alarms, doorbells and telephones ... and do so much more. If Shelly got it right, every home in the world would have a ShellyParrot. But not if they malfunctioned all the time.

Ricardo laughed nervously. "Interesting fact: the mouse is actually a robot-hamster. It appears to have deployed a set of complex movements. A sort of dance."

"A dance?"

"Yes, you know, people moving their bodies in rhythm—"

"I know what a dance is!" Shelly screeched.
Not that she would ever engage in something so
pointless. She watched Asha and Nush dance all
the way back to the zip line and whizz out of the
building. "It would be such a shame if the best
robots in the world didn't understand something as
simple as ... a dance."

"We have tried," said Ricardo. "But dancing is
a complicated human behaviour that's difficult to
predict."

"Tried," said Shelly, a look of distaste curling
over her upper lip. "You know I hate that word."
Her phone pinged with a FaceSpace notification.

"Ooh," she whimpered like she was in
real physical pain. "I lost a follower. Who is
loveshelz987? Why did they unfollow me? Was it
something I did? Too many hashtags? Not enough?
I feel sick."

Ricardo rushed forward to fan her.

"Get away from me," Shelly said, flinching.
"Do something useful and find out absolutely
everything you can about these two little girls.

I want a report on my desk by 6 a.m."

She stood up and took a deep breath in. That felt better. What was the mantra her life coach had given her? "I am in control, I have fresh breath, I am the best," Shelly whispered. "Control, fresh breath, best." Good, this was working.

"Now, where were we?" Shelly asked.

"We've still got sight of the suspects. They're in slow-moving traffic heading south-west. It looks like they are in a library van, reading books. There's an otter on the outside of the van but no other significant markings. We are within range, awaiting orders." Ricardo cleared his throat.

A library van. Shelly remembered how much she'd loved to read when she was Asha's age. She and her best friend, Giti, would pore over books for hours on end, reading their favourite passages... *Yuk!* Shelly shook herself out of her daydream. The past was in the past. Shelly was all about the future.

"Shall we bring them in for questioning? Or report them to the police for trespassing? Or we could book her a one-way ticket to Panama?" Ricardo continued.

"Rickybae, what a rich imagination you have!" Shelly smiled. Ricardo glowed. Then her smile disappeared, and she stared straight through him.

"None of the above."

She looked up at a self-portrait on the wall behind Ricardo. Gazing at herself helped Shelly to think. Asha's little exploits were certainly impressive.

But Shelly didn't need the police. She could get Asha exactly where she needed her to be, without lifting a finger.

"Get all of the third-floor security footage up on the big screen again. I want every angle." Ricardo started tapping frantically on his phone and the screen blinked into life.

Shelly watched the footage at triple speed for a few minutes, studying the screen like a hawk. "There!" she whooped, pointing at Asha and Drone on the third floor. "Ricardo, zoom in on that bit." Asha was standing in front of the Cyber Oak, swiping through document after document.

"So, she's snooping through all our plans, is she? Why isn't the Cyber Oak secure? Not even password protected." Shelly spoke so quietly and slowly that Ricardo had to stop breathing just to hear her.

"It's Claude from Security's fault, she's an idiot," Ricardo said quickly. He was sweating. "I am going to have a very strong word with her, Shelly. She's let herself down, she's let me down and worst of all, she's let you down. If I never—"

"I'll deal with it later," Shelly cut in. "This little girl must be trying to mess with our launch. And it looks like her sister is in on it too. Get me total access to their FaceSpace accounts, and their entire network: friends, family, everything."

Her eyes narrowed. "Let's bring these cuties down."

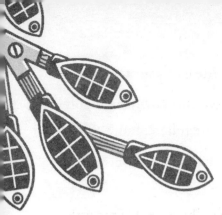

Chapter 10

.-- . / .-.. --- ...- . / - .-. .- .. -. ... -.-.--

21:16

"Welcome aboard this Caledonian Sleeper service to Inverness," a crackly voice called out through a speaker in their cabin. It was right in Asha's ear. She winced. "My name's Mark, and I'm your host. The dining car is now open. Find it towards the centre of the train."

"Excellent," said Drone. "It's been 4 hours and 21 minutes since you ate."

Asha was opening drawers, flicking switches and undoing all the different straps and catches in the cabin. She lifted the top of the table and found a little basin underneath. Another dead end.

"There's got to be some kind of spy switch in here, Hedy said this was the CSA cabin."

"I'm pretty sure it's just a regular cabin," said Nush, flipping through a magazine she'd found in the welcome pack.

Asha found a catch high up on the wall and wiggled it free.

THUNK!

The wall folded down, knocked Asha over and stopped a centimetre above Nush's head.

"ASHA! Be careful!" said Drone, fussing around

them as Asha got up to see what she'd discovered. It was a fold-down bed.

"Wheeeee!" Tumble howled, swinging himself from the blind onto the top bunk. He tipped out the rest of the contents of the welcome pack. He opened up a menu card, turned it over and crawled in. His head popped out the other side, his back feet still wiggling. "A micro-tent! Very spy."

Even Nush smiled. Asha grabbed the pillow and held it over her head, giggling. "Oooo-oooooh I'm the pillow-head. I've come to steal your dreeeaaaammmsss!"

"Not the pillow-head!" said Nush, yelping as Asha got close. They used to play this all the time. Tumble started filming, adding a running commentary. "Wassup, fannos? It's T-time and you're watching 'Behind the Scenes with the Joshis'." He winked at the camera.

Nush pulled a towel over her head and crouched, floating her arms around. "And I'm the ghooooost of lost towels!" They fell about laughing. Asha and Nush hadn't done this in so long.

"Nush, quiet," said Asha suddenly. "I think I can hear something." Nush gulped. Tumble froze. He was still filming. "Is that...? It can't be..." Asha leaned over, straining to hear. "...THE FARTING MACHINE!" She let out a huge fart, aimed straight for Nush's nose.

"Asha!" Nush coughed, laughing, tears coming to her eyes.

"Perfection," said Tumble, who had caught it all on camera. "Nush, I just sent it to you."

Nush opened her phone and started watching the video on a loop. "This is hilarious! Your farts are death!"

Asha walked over and shoved her little finger in front of Nush's screen. "Hey! Promise not to share."

"Of course, pinkie promise," said Nush, hooking her own little finger onto her sister's.

Over Asha's shoulder, Nush noticed something strange. The door handle had a card slot in it, like a hotel door, and there was a small otter engraved on its surface.

"Do you have that card thingy you used in the van?" Nush asked, walking towards the door.

"Sure, but I doubt the CSA would be that obvious," Asha said, taking the card out of a hidden zip-pocket in her sleeve and handing it over. Nush put the card in the slot, waited for a second, then pulled it out. Nothing happened.

"See!" Asha said smugly.

Nush rolled her eyes at her sister and wiped the card on her jeans. Then she blew sharply inside the card holder, put the card back in and jiggled it around. A little green light flashed, the door clicked and a burst of white light dazzled everyone.

"No WAY!" said Asha. "You found it!"

The room had transformed. The bunk beds had flipped back, and somehow the cabin had doubled in size.

"Never forget that I am much older and wiser than you." Nush winked at Asha.

Asha felt like she'd died and gone to gadget heaven. She looked around, her eyes wide with excitement. Every wall was covered in gear and equipment, on hooks and shelves and rotating platforms. There were things with rockets, things that hovered, things that glowed.

On the wall closest to them were raincoats, five types of compass, a little orange whistle and...

"Scarves!" said Drone, zooming over to inspect

their warmth-to-weight ratio. "You'll need one of these, Asha. You know how your neck gets chilly."

"Sure." Asha wasn't listening. On the wall, she saw a set of climbing equipment. She stuffed it into her bag, along with a few energy bars.

"Take this too, Asha," said Drone, pointing to a head net. "You might need to prevent an attack of Culicoides impunctatus."

"Culico-what?"

"Midges," Drone clarified.

"Tiny biting insects found in almost every environment on earth," said Tumble. Everyone looked at him. "It's on 'The Orkney Factor'." He shrugged.

Asha spotted a tall glass cabinet to the far right of the cabin. It was full of gadgets. Bingo! She unclipped the door's latch and suddenly all of the lights switched off. Hedy beamed into the room, taking the form of a giant midge.

"Ew," said Nush.

MY MISSIONS   **MY TRAINING**   **MY INTEL**

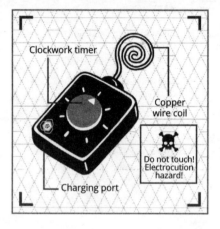

Clockwork timer

Copper wire coil

Do not touch! Electrocution hazard!

Charging port

EMP-ENDER

WARNING: This gadget is an electromagnetic pulse generator and is illegal in most countries. ONLY USE WITH PERMISSION.
Once detonated, the EMP-Ender will create a powerful pulse of electromagnetic energy that will temporarily disable all electronic devices within ten metres.

DANGER. DO NOT put the EMP-Ender next to anything electrical.

CSA CLIMBING GEAR

CSA-issue climbing gear is super light, uber-strong and has extra padding for unexpected falls. Remember to follow climbing safety protocols: Ensure your harness is a snug fit and tie on properly with a figure of eight and stopper knot.

Click **here** for information on the CSA's Global Climbing Competition.

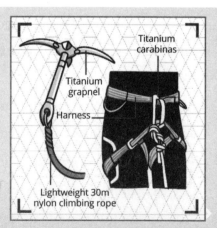

Titanium carabinas

Titanium grapnel

Harness

Lightweight 30m nylon climbing rope

MY MISSIONS | MY TRAINING | MY INTEL

Sensor

Warnings

Wind speed turbine

SAFE ⊕

CO2 0.4% N2 78%
CO   O 21%
CH4   H2O 0.5%

Mode buttons

Screen – shows composition of air (includes extra-sensitivity to toxic farts)

MAGI-NOSE

A hand held device for measuring air quality and whether it's safe to breathe.

The Magi-Nose can detect lack of oxygen, excessive carbon dioxide, carbon monoxide, methane, asbestos, potent farts, deadly farts, mild farts, extreme high or low humidity and even wind speed.

INTERNAL USE ONLY

COPYCAT CARD

This can copy any RFID signature and open *any* keycard lock. The processor scans for nearby RFID signatures and clones them so that it can function like a "skeleton key" for RFID keycard locks. It contains a microprocessor (a tiny computer) and must be kept charged.

Note: (1) Not a debit or credit card – you cannot use it to buy ice cream. **(2)** Not to be used to scrape ice off windows, cars or skis.

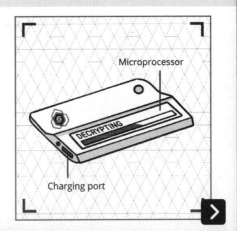

Microprocessor

DECRYPTING

Charging port

›

"Greetings, Agent Asha. Anushka Avani Joshi, you have been detected for the second time."

Asha scowled at Nush.

"I am here to give you gadget instructions and a mission update. We have discovered that Shelly suffers from sidonglobophobia."

"Erm, cool, thanks for letting me know." Asha rolled her eyes at Nush, who shrugged.

Hedy's hologram floated towards Asha. "That raincoat is part of the recommended kit list for your Scottish mission," continued Hedy. "Along with thermal pants and the Magi-Nose."

Asha spotted a nose-shaped device. "It analyses the amount of carbon monoxide, carbon dioxide, methane and other gases in the air," said Hedy.

"Very cool, thanks, Hedy," Asha said, trying to hide her disappointment. "I just wondered if I might need more than a raincoat and a nose thing to bring down a whole server farm." She scanned the cabinet. "Like, maybe... Do you have a server-farm-bringer-downer?"

"Negative."

"What about this?" Asha said, pointing to a small metal ring with loads of tiny lights inside.

"Negative. That is a microbiome ring, for sewer-related missions."

"Gotcha. And that one?" Asha pointed to a smooth device that looked like a barcode scanner.

"Negative. That is a robot guide dog for visually impaired agents," Hedy replied.

Asha carried on looking. There must be something in there that she could use. Asha crouched down to see what was on the bottom shelf and came face to face with a big red sign:

> **NOT TO BE USED EXCEPT IN
> EXTREME CIRCUMSTANCES BY ANY AGENT.
> EXPLICIT LEVEL 10 CSA PERMISSION NEEDED.
> DO NOT TOUCH. DANGER. THIS DEVICE
> IS ILLEGAL IN MOST COUNTRIES.**

Next to the sign, there was a small, clunky-looking black box with a wind-up timer on the front, like the dial from a really old oven. On one side, Asha could see a loop of copper wiring. A second sign read: WARNING: ELECTROMAGNETIC PULSE GENERATOR. ILLEGAL. DO NOT GET CAUGHT WITH IT OR LEAVE IT LYING ON THE BUS.

"Hedy, what does this do?"

"That is an electromagnetic pulse generator. It is extremely dangerous. If you set it off, it will produce a zap of energy that has the power to destroy all electronic devices in range. All computers and robots would stop working, and their insides would melt irreversibly."

"DANGER! DANGER! RISK OF DEATH! EMP WITHIN RANGE!" Drone's high-alert pixels started flashing as she buzzed around frantically.

"It is an exceptionally potent weapon and is only authorized for use in the most extreme of circumstances," Hedy continued. "Simple, sturdy equipment and your own brain is all you need, Asha. The rest of these items are strictly off-limits."

Asha looked at the EMP-Ender for a second longer. It was really small for something so powerful – it could fit neatly into the palm of her hand.

"Got it, Hedy. I won't touch that thing." Asha looked at the floor and stuffed her hands inside her pockets, crossing her fingers.

"The vote is in less than eighteen hours. You need to stay focused: break into ShellyPlex, shut down the spambots and get out."

"OK, thanks. I won't let you down, Hedy. I promise that this time—"

Hedy vanished as she was mid-sentence. Asha took her hands out of her pockets, yawned loudly and stretched her arms as high as they could go.

"Your optimal sleep time has passed," Drone noted. "Approximately 1 hour 23 minutes ago."

"Totally," said Asha. "You wash your face first," she said, nudging Nush. "Oh and, Drone, do you know if the mattress has a fire retardant layer on it?"

"Excellent question!" Drone beeped. "Let me check."

While Nush dribbled soapy water into the sink, and Drone checked the flammability of the bedding, Asha returned to the gadget cabinet. The EMP-Ender sat behind the glass. It was very small for something so powerful. Hedy had said not to take it because it was dangerous, but Shelly was dangerous too. Who knew what she might do to Asha when no one was looking? It would be good to have protection. Then again, Hedy's warning had sounded even more serious than usual.

"Smelly-face, where's your tooth-brushing game?" Tumble's voice made Asha jump. "Come join us at the sink-io."

"Yep, coming." Asha's cheeks burned a little as she made her way to the cabin sink. The sisters

brushed their teeth together, climbed into bed and switched off the lights. The room filled with the blue glow of their screens.

"Put them down!" Drone said, sternly whirring from Asha to Nush to Tumble as they scrolled. "Exposure to blue light disrupts your circadian

rhythms, resulting in reduced quality of sleep which can impact on reaction time, endurance and problem-solving skills!"

They put their phones away, but were too excited to sleep. Nush and Asha talked for hours about the day, and Operation Cyber Chop, the dens they used to make, and how hairy their dad's neck was. When Drone reminded them that it was two in the morning and she was putting herself on charge, they were swapping jokes about beans.

As Asha was finally drifting off to sleep, Nush whispered up to her, "I'm sorry I snitched on you so much to Mum and Dad. Let's stick together from now on... You're actually pretty cool for a little sister."

Asha smiled down at Nush, who looked like a kidney bean, curled up under a blanket. "You're pretty cool for a big sister too."

"You're the best sisters in the world," Tumble joined in, wiping a fake tear from his eyes. "Goodnight, fam. Sweet dreams."

As they slept to the soft clacka-di-clack of the

train, Asha's tablet started to glow in the darkness.

A notification appeared on the screen. Then another. And another. And another and another and another. Then a whole blur as 77,654 more notifications flooded in.

And they said exactly the same thing:
#Asha_is_a_stinkybomb_machine
#AshaPoopyPants

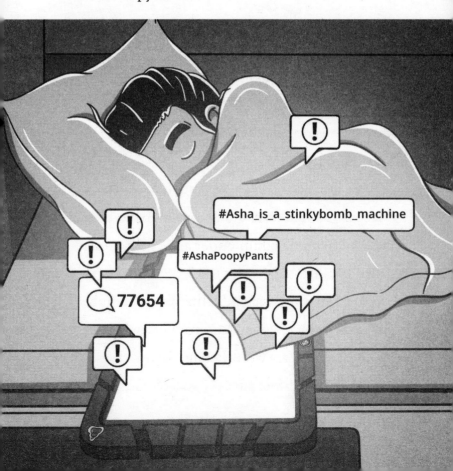

Chapter 11

.- ... .- / .. ... / -. --- - / .- / .--. --- ---
.--. -.-- -....- .--. .- -. - ... .-.-.-

August 08 - 07:40

CLANK. Bright lights. "Wakey-wakey!" yelled
a voice in the corridor. CLANK CLANK. The
banging was getting louder. "Everybody up!" Their
door rattled.

"It's a gorgeous day in the Highlands!" The
voice was so loud it could be inside Asha's pillow.
She squinted one eye open. Nush groaned and
pulled the covers over her ears. "We'll arrive at
Inverness in 2 minutes. All change please."

It took Asha a second to remember where she
was, and another second to blink her eyes into
focus. The first thing she saw was Drone, hovering

5 centimetres from her nose.

"ASHA AND ANUSHKA JOSHI! We have approximately 4 minutes to reach our connecting train!" Drone had her extra-loud setting on. She had been trying to wake them up since dawn. "3 minutes 56 seconds now."

"WHAT!" the sisters cried in unison. They'd overslept. "Chalo!" Asha yelled, poking Tumble awake and dashing out of the door with Nush, shoelaces half tied.

"Wait – my backpack!" Asha dashed back to the cabin, grabbed her bag and ran back to find Nush talking to a man in a hi-vis vest.

"You'll be wanting platform 2, wee lassie!" he said, helpfully.

Asha forced a smile and grabbed her sister. They ran for the train, jumping through the doors just as they were beeping shut.

"Phew, that was close!" said Nush, sitting down at a table seat.

"You shouldn't be talking to anyone," Asha scolded her in a tense whisper. "We're on an official CSA mission and we don't know who we can trust."

"Are you serious? I literally just asked him where the train to Orkney was. Which, by the way, is not even a thing. We actually need to go to Thurso and get the shuttle bus to the ferry and then…"

"I already knew that," Asha snapped. "We're undercover. You can't talk to anyone about what we're doing!"

"It's OK. Talk to me when you've got over your

morning baby grumps," said Nush. She rolled up her jumper as a pillow, leaned against the window and shut her eyes.

Tumble hopped out onto the table and started vlogging. "Morning, peeps. It's a fresh 7 a.m. and time for the morning insights and trends. First up: where are we at with MC Dog? Next: why did DJ-B tag herself in Orkney yesterday? Follow, like and discuss in the comments below."

Tumble was interrupted by a ping from Asha's backpack. Asha took out her tablet to find a stream of notifications. She opened one and hit "play". It was the video of Asha farting from last night, and there were thousands of comments on it. It had been shared by practically everyone she knew on FaceSpace, all using the same hashtag: #AshaPoopyPants. Asha's stomach lurched.

"Whoa, OMG, Asha! Wow! Have you seen FaceSpace this morning?" exclaimed Tumble, scrolling through his own phone. "It's on fire. And it's all about you. Your school is involved, your fam... You've even got your own top-trending hashtag, #AshaPoopyPants… It's been picked up on Wolf News. Here, look!"

Tumble shared his screen, pointing to the headline: "Exclusive footage shows tree-sceptic farting girl has no shame," Tumble read. "Oh look, they talk about your outfit too, and your eyebrows."

Asha started to panic. Not about her outfit or her eyebrows or her family – they knew she farted all the time. She didn't care about being called a "tree-sceptic" either. She was panicking about the CSA. Just the fact that the video had been shared was bad enough – agents all over the world would never take her seriously again. But the anonymity of the CSA might be under threat too. What if someone could trace it back to them? Asha took a breath, but it came out as a sob. Her tablet pinged again.

"Sorry, that's just me," said Tumble, not looking up. "My followers need my view on all this." He flicked on his camera and held his phone up, zooming in on Asha's face. "I'm here with #AshaPoopyPants and we're taking a moment to let it all sink in. I'm as shocked as you are. Stay tuned for more."

"Tumble, not now," said Asha. Tumble saw her face and put his phone down. She looked straight at him. "Did YOU post that video?"

"Asha! Never! I'd use a much better filter. Plus, I can't post anything unless you approve it first – remember! Silly sausage. If you scroll to the top, I think you'll find it's—" Tumble pretended to zip his mouth shut and dramatically pointed across the table.

"NUSH!" Asha screamed. A few people in their carriage looked up.

"What?" said Nush, who was still dozing against the window. "Can you chill?!"

"CHILL?" yelled Asha. She was trying not to cry, but it wasn't working. "After what you've done?!"

"I literally haven't done anything!" said Nush.

"Oh yeah, what about this?" said Asha, slamming her tablet up to Nush's face.

Asha was staring at her sister. "You made a pinkie promise! I trusted you!"

Nush looked at the post. "It wasn't me, I swear!"

"At least own up to it," said Asha through her tears.

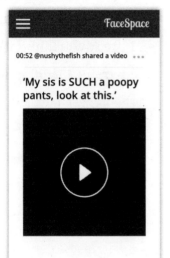

"You're a huge fake. You just want to impress your stupid friends, and get stupid likes, and now you've put the whole mission in danger. You always make everything about you. You don't care about the climate or about trees or our park." Asha took a deep breath. "And you do *not* care about me one bit."

Nush looked stunned. "Well, now you know how I felt this morning when you ruined my internship," she said defensively.

"I can't look after you both if you're fighting," Drone beeped, panicking. She whirred from Asha to Nush and back again. "I'm sure there's a perfectly reasonable explanation for the post. Asha, the FaceSpace terms and—"

"Thanks, Drone, but I really don't care," interrupted Asha. Her ears were hot. "I just need to get away from *her*." Asha grabbed her backpack and stomped to a seat further down the carriage.

"The risks to sibling wellbeing grow exponentially if you don't learn to resolve conflict. I estimate mission success is 78 per cent less likely if you two don't resolve your differences. Let's go back over there and make a talking circle," Drone suggested.

Tumble trotted after her. "Asha, this is a proper crisis situation. It's like when celebs go rogue and get a spokesperson, a life coach, and a slot on national TV."

Asha ignored them both. She clenched her fists and ground her teeth. She'd never been so angry, hurt or ashamed. Nush had deliberately sabotaged her. How could she have put the whole mission – the whole of the CSA – in danger? Asha frowned out of the window, watching the faint reflection of her face slide over the flat brown landscape beyond.

Tumble changed tack. "What about a quiz? Everybody cheers up with a quiz!"

Drone beeped her approval and loaded ORKNEY FUN FACTS. "There are very few trees on Orkney. Why?"

"Because Shelly killed them all?" Asha sulked.

"Incorrect," said Drone. "It's a mixture of early humans chopping them down around 3,500 years

ago, plus climatic factors. It's too damp and windy."

"Windy? You should fit right in, poopy-pants!" said Tumble, leaning over to one side to let out an imaginary fart. Asha didn't respond. Not even a flicker. This must be bad.

"Next question," said Drone quickly. "How many ferries are there to Orkney?"

"Pah! That's easy. Trick question, 'ferries'! There must be only ONE!" said Tumble proudly.

"Incorrect! There are actually four routes," beamed Drone, eager to discuss transport options. "The shortest route is between John O'Groats..." Tumble already looked bored. Drone fell silent. They both looked at Asha, who was still scowling.

This was going to be a long journey.

Chapter 12

.. - .-..-. ... / -. --- - / --- ...- . .-. / -.-- . -
-.-.--

07:54

About 500 miles away, Ricardo hurried into Shelly's
office, looking flustered but excited.

"You're late," Shelly snarled, inspecting her nail-
beds. "I would so hate for that to be a stain on your
record." She looked up. "Tell me you've got good
news."

"We're getting serious traction for the Cyber
Oak," said Ricardo, handing Shelly a full report
of the latest stories from the global newspapers.
"Everyone is ready for today's vote! They love the
Oaks. There were a few blogs from local residents
in Wembley whining about their park, but nothing

to worry about – we've buried those stories. We're headed for a landslide victory, and the green light for our global tree-shops!" He beamed.

"I think you mean our life-enhancing trees," said Shelly. She was extra spiky this morning. "And the two girls? I assume they're no longer a problem."

Ricardo smiled and tapped his tablet into life. "Our FaceSpace boost worked perfectly. With a little help from our cheeky spambots, the #AshaPoopyPants story went viral. Her family and friends think she's gross. They are falling right into our trap."

"Wonderful." Shelly looked satisfied. She was going to win. And not just one silly park in Wembley. Soon she'd have a billion Cyber Oaks monitoring everyone's every move. She'd be able to track people all over the world.

"There's just one thing…" Ricardo paused.

"I don't like pauses, Ricky. What is it?"

"The girls are still on their way to Orkney. And, er, they might not know about the server farm, but…" said Ricardo. He saw the corners of Shelly's mouth twitch for a fraction of a second.

She took a deep breath. "Where are they, exactly?"

Ricardo swiped through a few screens on his tablet. "On a train. In the far north of Scotland. We tracked the older one – Anushka – easy enough when location services are enabled on FaceSpace!" Ricardo looked pleased with himself. "Shall I have someone meet them off the train? Bundle them into a car, drop them in the middle of nowhere?"

"That won't be necessary. I'd hate for you to get all stressed and make another one of your mistakes. Time to switch to plan B. Alert everyone at ShellyPlex."

Shelly's phone rang. She answered, and listened for a moment. "So you've made the ShellyParrot dancing update? Fabulous. Thank you, Dr Wade." She hung up, dialled another number and waited for it to connect.

A woman's voice answered. "DJ-B," said Shelly smoothly. "Hi. I'm expecting guests today – a couple of kids. Make them welcome, show them a few headline reports... Yes, VIP treatment. Keep them busy for me, just for a few hours. Thanks, my lovely!"

She turned back to Ricardo. "Get my jet ready."

"Er, it looks better for your followers if we make greener choices," Ricardo said hesitantly. "We could get the train?"

"It looks better for you, Ricardo, if you do as you're told." Shelly's mouth tightened into a thin line. "Book. My. Jet. Now."

Chapter 13

.- --. . -. - ... / .- .-. . / ... - .-. --- -. --. .
.-. / - --- --. . - .... . .-. .-.-.-

11:08

"LEAVE. ME. ALONE!" Asha yelled.

She was four steps ahead of Nush, on the
concrete ramp for the ferry. The bow of the ship
had risen up, opening like a ginormous mouth,
ready to gobble up the lorries, cars and caravans
waiting in neat lines in front of it.

Asha was still seething. The more Nush denied
posting the videos, the less Asha believed her.
Drone kept trying to soothe her, but she wasn't in
the mood.

"You're not a CSA agent," Asha snapped at Nush,
"and I don't need you getting in the way of my

mission. Stop following me."

"I'm not going to just leave you here," sighed Nush. "We're a long way from home. We have to stick together. We're sisters."

Asha spun around to face Nush. "I wish I didn't have a sister," she said. Then she saw the look on Nush's face and instantly regretted it.

"Fine. You know what?" Nush stood still. "Suit yourself. Go on your own."

"Yeah. I will." Asha stormed off towards the ferry.

"I don't need you or your silly little spy agency to uncover the truth!" Nush called after her. "I'm going to deal with DJ Bestlyfe, with or without you!"

"Great, go back to London and deal with your

precious DJ-B. Do whatever you want, just leave me alone!"

"DJ-B isn't in London; she's in Orkney too. She's got a whole DJ booth set up in the underground bunker at ShellyPlex and she's live-streaming her set tomorrow. Clearly you haven't been tracking her latest movements on FaceSpace. Not such a great spy after all!" Nush raised her eyebrows and smiled at Asha, unbearably smug.

"And you didn't even pick the fastest route to Orkney! Which is via Kirkwall, by the way. See you never, loser," Nush called, as she huffed off to a different terminal.

Drone was really worried now. She whirred over to Nush. "If I could just point you to Sub-Clause 14 of—"

"Leave her!" Asha snapped

"But, I just—"

"Drone, you're meant to look after me, remember?" said Asha, hardening her resolve to have nothing to do with Nush. Drone span in mid-air and followed Asha to the ferry.

It began to rain: just a light drizzle coming in off the grey sea. Asha shivered. Maybe she should have taken that scarf after all. She hurried up the ramp, stepped into the warmth of the ferry and looked for a quiet spot. She picked a huge squishy seat and stared glumly out of the window.

After forty minutes of total silence, Tumble couldn't bear it any more and cuddled in close. "Don't be sad, Asha! I'm sure we can get you back in the selfie game and no one will even remember this in a few years' time."

"Selfies?" replied Asha. "Tumble, I don't care about that. I just can't believe Nush would post that video. Do you remember when she was eleven, and Dad posted a picture of her dribbling in her sleep in the car? She refused to leave the house for two weeks. She just sat in her room and cried. And Dad only has five followers, and one of them's Mum! I can't believe her."

"Yeah, you should never post a video of a fart without the farter's permission," said Tumble wisely.

"I just don't know why she'd do that to me,

especially when we were having so much fun."

Asha's anger had turned into a sick feeling. It didn't make sense. She scrolled through the latest #AshaPoopyPants comments. It was weird that the whole thing had gone viral. Nush only had 37 followers and they were all people Asha knew. How could there be thousands of posts about it? Asha clicked on one. It looked fake. In fact, most of the people who were posting about #AshaPoopyPants looked fake. Just like DJ-B's followers.

Wait. Links started to form in Asha's mind. What if Shelly was somehow behind this too? She'd discovered Nush's hidden camera, and Ricardo had practically chased her out of Shelly HQ. If Shelly knew about Asha's investigations, maybe she wanted her and Nush to fight, just to distract them.

Tumble's phone pinged. "Oooh, Shelly B's just updated her FaceSpace." Tumble put on his best Shelly-Belly voice. "#CyberOak is trending in **A**ustria, **S**enegal, **H**aiti and **A**ndover. Once I set my mind to something, there's no stopping me!"

"Wait, show me that." Asha sat upright in her seat and read the post four times. The capital letters jumped out at her. Was she being paranoid, or was it a hidden message? Asha felt funny. She couldn't quite put her finger on it. Maybe it was trapped gas. Or maybe it was regret.

"Erm, guys." Asha gulped, finally. "What if it was Shelly, not Nush, who posted the video?"

"It is 98 per cent likely that Shelly posted it from Nush's FaceSpace account, which she is allowed to do under Clause 14 of the FaceSpace terms and conditions. I have tried to tell you 16 times!" Drone huffed.

"Oooh," said Tumble. "Sneaky!"

The truth finally hit Asha. She'd been wrong. And horrible. And now Nush was on her own, about to face the meanest, most powerful person Asha had ever met –  and with no spy training whatsoever.

Asha had forgotten the first and most important rule of the CSA: Question Everything. It was a rookie mistake to let your emotions cloud your judgement. Shelly had set up a trap, and Asha had sleepwalked into it.

Not for a second longer, she thought. Asha reached for her pad as a new plan started to form in her mind. She'd need to be even more careful than before, now that she knew Shelly was expecting her. But there was one thing Shelly wasn't expecting. Asha and Nush were not just best friends. They were family. Even when they screamed and shouted blue murder, they always made up. It was going to take more than the world's most powerful trillionaire to come between the Joshis.

"We're going to get Nush." Asha sounded determined. "And bring Shelly down."

"Totally," Tumble said, resting his paw on Asha's hand as Drone flew in close.

Asha's dreams of being an elite agent of the CSA faded into the background. And she didn't care about #AshaPoopyPants either.

She just had to find her sister.

Chapter 14

.--. .-.. .- -. / .. -. ...-. .. .-.. - .-. .- - .. ---
-. ... / -.-. .- .-. . ..-. .-.. .-.. -.-- .-.-.-

13:27

"Say nothing, speak to nobody, don't lick the floor."
Asha paused to look meaningfully at Tumble.

She was tucked away in a doorwell opposite the
ShellyPlex, watching the revolving entrance doors.
A cold blast of wind caught her hair.

Asha was running out of time and she needed
to use every second wisely. Nush had taken off
without giving Asha the chance to say sorry.
Luckily, Asha and Nush had shared a room for the
first eight years of Asha's life. Asha knew her sister
better than anyone. If Nush said she was going to
do something, she meant it. Asha was 99.9 per cent

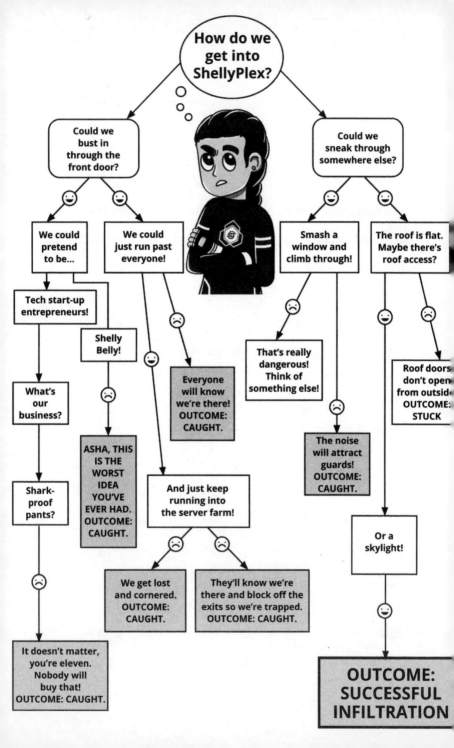

sure Nush was on her way to find DJ Bestlyfe and demand answers. That's where she would find her.

Hedy had made a brief appearance to check in on the mission and Asha chose not to mention Nush disappearing, or the #AshaPoopyPants hashtag going viral. She'd cut the conversation short by pretending to need a snack and had been jittery ever since.

But now that she was finally at ShellyPlex, ready to break in, Asha felt an unexpected sense of calm. She checked her notebook one final time.

* TOP SECRET *
Plan

Told ya!

Stage 1: First find Nush. (She'll be wherever DJB is.)

Stage 2: Head to the server farm. (FOUND)
It's LOCKED! Find key? Pick lock? Brute force? ???

Stage 3: Hack the spambots!
Use them to (spread the truth)

Stage 4: GET OUT!
Without dying
Save world, pass probation. YAY!

"Tumble, deploy Undercover-Toy-Mode test."

"Affirmative. Testing now," replied Tumble, who could barely contain his excitement. He froze his little features into a semi-smile and held his breath for four seconds, before gasping dramatically for air. "Toy Mode ready."

"Copy that," said Asha, smiling proudly at Tumble. "Drone, deploy Undercover-Delivery-Mode test."

"Affirmative," beeped Drone. And then using a different, cheese-grater, voice, "I am a delivery drone. I love deliveries! Did you order a pizza?"

She paused and then, returning to her normal voice, she said smoothly, "Test complete."

"Excellent," said Asha. "If we get into any trouble, you know what to do."

"Guys, this is SO EXCITING!" said Tumble, wriggling.

"Once we enter the ShellyPlex," said Drone, "we need to find the rooms underneath the main building. That's where the spambots will be, and the DJ booth too."

"Copy that," said Asha.

"Yeah, copy that, Robo-brains." Tumble winked at Drone and pointed across the street. "Come on, gang, the entrance is over there."

"Too risky!" said Asha. Instead, she dashed down an alleyway next to the main building and opened her backpack. She grabbed a climbing harness, unlooped a rope and aimed her grappling hook at the sky. "I've got a better idea."

"What are you doing?" Drone bleeped, warning lights flashing across her display.

Asha pressed a button, and the hook shot out of

her hands, screeching as it led the rope in a high arc up onto the roof. The hook bit into the tiles, and she tugged the rope taut.

"We can't just walk in, in broad daylight," replied Asha. "We'll have to break in through the roof."

"But the server farm is underground, Asha. We don't need to go on the roof!" Drone exclaimed.

"And I'm afraid of heights," Tumble added, burying his head in the backpack, his bum poking out.

"Shelly will be expecting us to try and break in at ground level. We need to launch a sneak attack." Asha fed the rope through the harness, and stuck CSA-issue sticky pads on to her feet, knees and hands. She gently pushed Tumble's bum further into her backpack and zipped it shut. "Chalo!"

Asha crawled up the wall as though gravity didn't exist, just like the geckos Nani-Ji had told her about. The higher she climbed, the faster her heart beat. She was a long way up, but laser-focused on the mission ahead.

At the top, Asha could see a huge skylight in the centre of the roof. It was open just a crack. Asha walked over and peered in. She could see an atrium below.

"The coast is clear," Asha whispered to Drone, as she lowered her rope down and held tightly on to it, swinging her bum over the edge. She pinched her eyes shut and slid all the way down to the floor. She'd made it!

Asha unbuckled the harness and roly-polied behind a bank of grey desks. This was nothing like the colourful playground at Shelly Inc HQ.

A lift dinged and two women walked out, holding tablets and muttering intensely. Asha held her breath, but they continued straight past her, barely looking up.

This was her chance! Asha floor-dived towards the lift, using the extra-slidey tummy patch on her bodysuit to glide through the doors.

"Welcome to the ShellyLift!" a robotic voice

boomed. "Where you can be yourself, but better. Which floor would you like?"

Tumble jumped out of Asha's backpack. "Bagsy!" he yelled, as he leapt to press the first button he could reach: BASEMENT. The lift descended at roller-coaster speed, and Asha felt her stomach lurch up her nose.

CLANK.

"You have reached your destination. Don't forget to punch today in the face!"

The doors opened and Asha stepped out into the basement. She saw that the ceiling, floor and walls were made of curved glass, filling the room with blue light. It felt like an aeroplane. Asha held her nose and squeezed her face, trying to make her ears pop. She rubbed her eyes and took a deep breath in.

It smelled strangely familiar: a slightly metallic, musty smell of solder, oil and plastic ... like the inside of a box of new computer parts. She could hear a low whirring sound, almost like when her computer overheated and the fan kicked in.

"Oh, my potatoes! Only a few hours until the vote and it looks like it's going to be a total landslide. I can't believe this!" Tumble's voice split the silence as he checked his phone.

Asha's stomach tightened in a knot of fury at the thought of Shelly getting away with this. "A world without real trees will be a total disaster," she agreed.

"Oh no, I'm not talking about that! I'm talking about MC Dog! He was in the lead, and then suddenly – puff! – everyone changed their mind! It's all over my FaceSpace! I don't think I can breathe. Help me, Drone!"

Asha rolled her eyes. How could Tumble be thinking about the "Show-Off" finals at a time like this? Her watch started to vibrate. Hedy had sent an update: the Cyber Oak had 26 million new likes on FaceSpace and #WonderfulWembley was trending. Asha pictured Wembley Park on a sunny day. She could see Nush climbing high into their favourite tree, shouting at Asha that she'd never be able to catch her. And now – no Nush, no trees, she was in the creepiest basement ever and she was pretty sure that Shelly was onto her. For the first time since this all started, Asha felt frightened.

Stop, Asha told herself. *Breathe.* She thought of Nani-Ji, who could always tell when Asha was getting overwhelmed and would whisper gently into her ear so that it tickled, "One step at a time, my little jalebi. Even the biggest journeys are made one step at a time."

One step at a time, thought Asha, moving forward. You just need to get to the DJ booth to find Nush. That's the next step.

Asha took a big step forward. And then another. And then another.

And then – BAM!

She walked headfirst into a big, gleaming silver signpost. To the left was the server farm. To the right was DJ-B's sound studio. Asha didn't have to think twice. She turned right. At the studio, she peered through a window in the door. DJ-B was inside, chatting to someone. Asha stood on her tiptoes and tried to get a glimpse of the person's face. She was a little shorter than DJ Bestlyfe, and she had shiny brown hair. From behind, she looked exactly like Asha's big sister.

Chapter 15

- .-. . . ... / ... . --- ..- .-.. -.. -. .-..-. - / -.
. . -.. / .--. .-.. ..- --. --. .. -. --. / .. -. .-.-.-

13:49

"NUSH! You're here! How did you get here
before me?" yelled Asha. She burst into the room
and ran full speed at her sister, almost toppling
her over. "I should never have said those horrible
things to you. I didn't mean them. I'm so sorry,"
she blubbed. "Shelly hacked into your FaceSpace
account! She's been onto us the whole time.
She was trying to make us argue to distract us,
and—"

"Save it, Asha. I'm so not interested," said
Nush firmly.

Asha's eyes brimmed with tears. Nush smirked

and gave her sister a gentle flick on the forehead.
"Just kidding. I still love you. I got here first
because I asked for DJ-B at reception and was taken
straight to her. Easy." Nush rolled her eyes at Asha.

"Getting all the feels!" DJ Bestlyfe's voice filled
the room as she walked over to Asha and stuck
out her hand. "I'm DJ Annie Bestlyfe, guest music
maker here at ShellyPlex. You can call me Annie!"
She was wearing a yellow tracksuit. She had the
same orange headphones draped around her neck
as always.

"Right, hi," said Asha, hesitantly.

"Whaaaaaat! LION!" Tumble whipped his phone out and switched the camera on.

"Oh, cute, a talking toy!" DJ Bestlyfe said as she leaned in and made a peace sign just in time for Tumble to snap a selfie.

"I'm a huge fan, the biggest!" Tumble exclaimed, and then launched into a speech about how he was training to be a DJ himself.

While Tumble waffled on, Asha looked around the room. It was impressive. Framed platinum discs covered the walls and there was a DJ booth with speakers towering on each side. Hundreds of dials, switches and blinking lights crowded around a huge screen, with a single laptop in the middle. Three Cyber Oak trees glowed at the back of the room.

Asha turned to her sister. "Nush, we need to get a move on. The vote is happening in less than two hours. The server room is just across the corridor." She went to take Nush's hand, but Nush was firmly planted to the floor.

"Actually, DJ-B and I have had a chat." Nush pointed to the glowing trees behind them. "She's shown me all the science and the Cyber Oaks are definitely good for the environment – just like Shelly's been saying all along." Nush's cheeks started to redden. She took a deep breath in. "I lost my internship because of your crazy theories, Asha."

"What?!" Asha replied, confused.

Nush placed a hand on her hip. "The Children's Spy Action Group, or whatever you're called, got the Cyber Oak majorly wrong."

Asha's stomach sunk a little, but she tried not to jump to conclusions this time. She needed to stay objective. "How do you know they are good for the environment?" Asha asked DJ-B.

"Shelly gave me this report herself." DJ-B started to rummage around in an oversized duffle bag on the floor, lifting a booklet out. "See!" DJ-B said, pointing at a bar graph inside showing a reduction in air pollution. "I wouldn't stick my name on fake news. No way!"

This couldn't be right. What about the whistle-blower Drone had found on the dark web, and the fake video of Nush, and the CSA's own report?

Asha looked at the graph. Then the small print on the bottom of the page caught her eye. It was based on a single test that had been carried out in Shelly's lab, far away from the natural world and any wildlife. Asha flicked through the rest of the report. It didn't have any information about the failed test sites in Orkney either. Typical.

Asha found the CSA report on her tablet, and showed it to DJ-B.

"The report Shelly's given you is super misleading. It's based on one Cyber Oak in a science lab. It doesn't include any of the tests she carried out in real life … in real parks! The Cyber Oak was shut down in Orkney because it injured loads of wildlife and polluted the air!"

Asha looked up, exasperated. That was

the problem with fake news. Even when the information was true, it might be less than half the story. Without all the facts, it was so hard to know what was real and what wasn't.

Nush raised her eyebrows and DJ-B let out a long sigh. Asha could see that she was going to need something more convincing to change their minds. She needed proof.

"Argh, fine! If you don't believe me, see for yourselves." Asha started walking towards one of the glowing Cyber Oaks at the back of the room. "These Oaks are on, right?"

"Yes," said DJ-B, breathing loudly through her nose. It's making the air in this studio

turbocharged. Don't you just feel super chill?"

Asha felt anything but chill. Her watch vibrated. There was less than an hour until the vote.

"Shelly has said that the trees store and use solar power, but this is plugged in."

"Well, we *are* underground," Nush pointed out.

Asha bent down to look at the plugs and the tree sprung into life. "**Good afternoon,**" it said. "**If you take a selfie with me, I'll reward you with 1,000 ShellyBucks.**" A purple light washed over Asha, as the tree scanned her from head to foot. "**It appears you deleted your FaceSpace account. Don't worry! I will create a new one for you.**"

"No!" said Asha. "Switch off!"

"**I do not understand that command. Would you like a new backpack? There's a 50 per cent flash sale on the ShellyGo! range.**"

Asha looked at DJ-B and Nush. "See! All the Cyber Oak does is encourage you to shop. It's not solar-powered." Asha moved in closer. There were loads of tiny hidden cameras nestled all over the tree, just like she had seen in Wembley Park. "And, worst of all, it's recording us all the time."

"I respect your privacy, Asha Joshi," the Cyber Oak said chirpily. "I have only recorded and stored these pictures to keep you safe." The tree displayed blown-up images of Asha bending over its base. "And I am not angry that you almost unplugged me, my friend!"

Nush's jaw dropped wide open.

"Are you sure? Like, perhaps your report could be wrong?" DJ Bestlyfe asked Asha, quietly this time.

"I can prove it. You say the Cyber Oak has been on all day, right?"

DJ-B nodded.

"I'll test the air." Asha pulled the Magi-Nose from a side pocket and waved it around in the air. After a few seconds, it beeped. Everyone looked at the screen. The air quality was really poor.

"SEE! It's a big scam!"

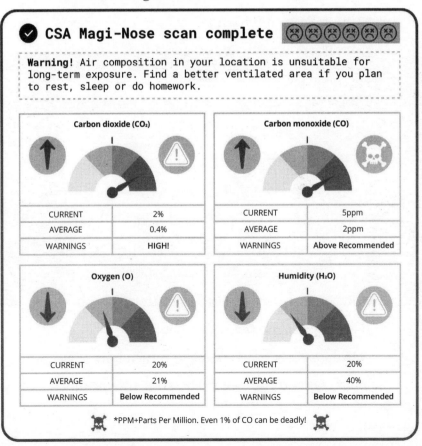

CSA Magi-Nose scan complete

Warning! Air composition in your location is unsuitable for long-term exposure. Find a better ventilated area if you plan to rest, sleep or do homework.

Carbon dioxide (CO_2)

CURRENT	2%
AVERAGE	0.4%
WARNINGS	HIGH!

Carbon monoxide (CO)

CURRENT	5ppm
AVERAGE	2ppm
WARNINGS	Above Recommended

Oxygen (O)

CURRENT	20%
AVERAGE	21%
WARNINGS	Below Recommended

Humidity (H_2O)

CURRENT	20%
AVERAGE	40%
WARNINGS	Below Recommended

*PPM+Parts Per Million. Even 1% of CO can be deadly!

DJ Bestlyfe's eyes looked like they might fall out. "This is cray, cray," she exclaimed loudly. "Shelly's been lying to me all this time!"

"Not just you – me too… She's been lying to everyone," Nush replied.

DJ Bestlyfe took five deep nasal breaths, and closed her eyes. When she opened them again, she had a very different look in her eyes. She turned to Asha.

"We're 100 p-cent going to sort this, big boom style. We'll get the truth to our peeps at double-trouble speed! We can bosh this! LION!" DJ-B broke into her famously wide smile.

"LION!" Tumble yelled.

"Great, I've got a plan," Asha said quickly, taking out her notebook. "Shelly is using spambots to spread the fake news. We can use the same bots to spread the truth to millions of people all over the world. And as soon as people see the truth, they won't vote 'yes' for the Cyber Oak."

DJ-B didn't need a second to think about it. "I'm in. What d'you need? My wheels? My limited-edition fragrance – for the vibes? Maybe some banging tunes?"

"I need to get into that room over there." Asha pointed across the corridor to the server farm. "And I need you to post about this on FaceSpace."

"Can do!" A notification appeared in the corner of DJ-B's screen. "We've got a little problem, my boomboxes…" DJ-B frowned. "Shelly's on her way down. Soz."

"We're doomed!" Tumble cried, clinging to Asha's leg.

"Hide behind that speaker. I've got this." DJ-B winked at the gang.

Crouching together at the back of the room, they heard footsteps first, then a smooth voice. "DJ Bestlyfe, so fab to see you. How are my little guests doing? Have you kept them busy for me?"

Shelly had arrived.

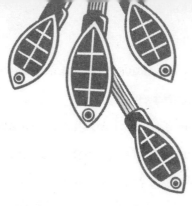

Chapter 16

.-.. . - .-..-. ... / --. --- / -- . --. .- -....- ...-
.. .-. .- .-.. -.-.--

14:22

"Shelly, it's been mad time! How's tricks?" DJ Bestlyfe had opened the door a crack, and Asha and Nush could see a small slice of Shelly from behind the speaker. Amanda rested on her shoulder and Ricardo was hovering behind.

"Fabulous." Shelly peered in.

"But I will be even more fabulous when I find those Joshi sisters."

"Hey, Shelly..." began DJ Bestlyfe, thinking on her feet. "Awkward, but you got any mints?"

"No. Why?"

"It's just... Did you have garlic at lunch?"

"No, I had a squash salad with caramelized red-onion hummus..." Shelly trailed off in horror. "I don't have the freshest breath?" Her voice rose at the end. Something did stink, that was for sure.

Asha wished she could see Shelly's face in the tense silence that followed. It felt like a full minute.

"Don't sweat, lovely. We can fix this," breezed DJ Bestlyfe. "Bathroom is over there. Remember the first rule of fresh breath: three-minute brush, five-minute floss, a lifetime of dazzle. LION!"

"Thanks!" whispered Shelly. Asha heard footsteps as she hurried away.

"Quick, let's go to the server room." DJ-B beckoned to Asha and Nush.

They tiptoed across the corridor and Asha swiped her CSA Copycat Card across a huge digital lock.

It clicked, the doors opened and the gang piled through. There were rows of computers as far as the eye could see, stacked from the floor to the ceiling, all blinking tiny green lights. Tumble shivered. It was cold and dark inside. Behind the door, Asha spotted a desk and a laptop with a big gold Shelly Inc sticker on the front. That must be the control desk. Asha sat down and the laptop glowed into life.

"Here's the plan. DJ-B, we need to write a FaceSpace post from your account and tell everyone the truth. I'll code the spambots to make your posts go viral. And then we'll get out of here."

Nush gave Asha a gooey look like she was impressed. It felt weird. Asha was more used to Nush's dagger eyeballs.

"Totally!" DJ-B handed her phone over to Nush. "I'll keep watch for Shelly. You better whoosh though!"

Asha nodded. She was already getting into the zone. "Nush, can you post from DJ-B's account? And use the hashtag #CyberChop."

"Sure," Nush whispered, fingers flying over the keyboard as she typed.

FaceSpace

@nushythefish shared a post

Remember. DO NOT VOTE "YES" to the Cyber Oak! Explosive report just discovered about Shelly Inc. **Here** are the highlights. Click **here** for the full report on freescienceresistance.org! #CyberChop

@nushythefish shared a post

Warning! The Cyber Oaks are cyber WRONG. They damage ecosystems, hurt wildlife and make our planet even warmer. It's all fake news. The science is all **here**. DO NOT VOTE "YES" FOR THEM.

"Tumble, can you tag the biggest influencers?"

"YES-IY-O!" Tumble shouted. Whispering wasn't his thing.

"Drone, can you plan our route out of here?" Asha continued.

"Copy that," Drone robo-whispered back.

"Now for the coding part..."

Tumble's Totes Cool Guide to Going Mega-Viral

Step 1: Make a post they can't ignore!

Numbered lists! Emotional wording! Makes you part of the "cool club" who are in the know.
Faces with BIG expressions!

LIKE THIS

8 mind-blowing facts about Cyber Oaks Shelly Belly doesn't want you to know!

Step 2: Tag influencers and use hashtags to get seen!

@Sophiedeen
@Famousscientist
#climatechange #abetterworld

Step 3: Post and engage with responses!

I post...
Their followers share...
Their followers share...

My followers share...

VIRAL, YO!

The gang fell silent as they all got to work. Asha opened the terminal on the computer using DJ-B's login and started hunting for the spambots programme. Within seconds, lines of code had filled the screen. Asha's eyes jumped from tag to tag, and the room seemed to dissolve behind her as she hunted for the right bit. There! She'd found it.

Asha tweaked the code and watched it finish compiling. Once everyone found out the truth, there was no way people would vote to have Cyber Oaks in Wembley Park. Asha could feel the adrenaline in her fingers as she hit "RUN".

"I've done it!" She jumped up.

"Mission complete! Now let's get out of here!"

"LION!" Tumble and DJ-B said in unison, while Drone beeped her approval. Only Nush held back. Something was wrong.

"Erm, guys, sorry to be a downer, but when Shelly finds out, can't she just use the spambots to spread the fake news again?" Nush paused.

Asha's heart sank. Her sister was right.

"I think we need to shut the spambots down, for good," Nush added.

DJ-B looked from Nush to Asha and back to Nush again. "We're talking 60 seccos before Shelly returns. What's plan B?"

They were almost out of time. Asha had a thought. It was dangerous, but it might just work. She reached down and felt along the inside of her hidden pocket. It had been digging into her ribs ever since they got off the overnight train, but Asha felt too bad to tell anyone. She had promised herself she'd return it as soon as she could.

Asha carefully removed the EMP-Ender from her bodysuit and held it up in the palm of her hands. As soon as Drone set her pixellated eyes on it, she started screeching at her highest volume.

"DANGER! DANGER! RISK OF DEATH!"

"OMG. OMG. DANGER!" Tumble immediately joined in.

"Shhh! Calm down!" Asha stuck her finger over her mouth. "Shelly will hear us!"

"If you set that death machine off, Shelly will be the last thing we need to worry about. You won't just shut the spambots down. You will also destroy me, Tumble and everything around us that uses a computer," Drone beeped frantically. "It is a fatal weapon!"

"But there's no other way to stop the spambots! And I can set the timer so we won't be here when it detonates. You'll be fine!"

Asha was interrupted by the sound of footsteps heading towards them. She only had a few seconds to make up her mind. She looked at the little object in her hand. There were 60 minutes on the timer. Surely that was enough time to get far, far away from the server room. Drone and Tumble wouldn't be in any danger. And how else could she stop Shelly? She had to do something – the planet was at stake.

The footsteps came to a halt.

"Psst!" DJ Bestlyfe stuck her head out of the door. "Over here."

"Love that clove-flavour toothpaste, DJ-B! I knew you weren't a peppermint scrub!" Shelly's voice was muffled from behind the door.

"Aha! Scrub! You're a riot. Looking and smelling f-to-the-resh! I love your shoes, by the way..."

Shelly suddenly became very still. "Why are you in the server room?" she asked. Then she muttered through gritted teeth, "Did Ricardo give you access?"

"I got lost looking for you!" DJ-B said chirpily. "But here you are! Yay! Quick selfie?"

DJ-B manoeuvred herself into the doorway.

"Your job is to make the Cyber Oak look good.
Not nose around in places that you're not meant to
be." Shelly's lip twitched.

"Actually, Shellz, my job is to create boom
music. It's a skill that's taken me forevs to master."
DJ-B carried on smiling, but something had
hardened in her eyes.

"Yes, yes, sure." Shelly swatted away at the air.
"Look, I've paid you to be the face of the Cyber Oak
campaign. So be a good face, won't you, and move
out of my way." Shelly tried to move past DJ-B.

"Hear this, Shellzio. I only agreed to represent the
Cyber Oak because I believed your lies." DJ-B stood
firm.

"Excuse me?" Shelly said slowly.

"That's right. I know the truth."

"Oh, sweetie, you haven't been listening to those
two little girls, have you? I thought DJs were meant
to have good taste." Shelly smiled as she spoke.
"Sure, we haven't got the science perfect yet, but
that's what updates are for. What's important now

is that we get those Cyber Oaks voted in. Let me worry about the details. Ricardo! Get here now!"

"No, no, no, that's not the flow, flow, flow. You're tricking the public to get them to buy, buy, buy, but it's not going to fly, fly, fly." DJ-Bestlyfe was trying to stall Shelly.

Shelly scowled. "I'm providing an essential service. People love shopping, and I'm just helping them to shop in one of their favourite places – parks. I'm doing you all a favour, and you just don't know it yet. Now, stop wasting my time and get out of the way," she said in a low voice. "Right now."

"Do it!" shouted Asha.

As DJ Bestlyfe stepped aside, Shelly's face cracked into a wild grin as she locked eyes with Asha. "I've got you—"

"NOW!" shouted Asha, clicking her heels

together, triggering Flashbang Mode. Her shoes made a very high-pitched electronic shriek and then sent out a dazzling light. Ricardo and Shelly were blinded and deafened at the same time, losing all sense of where they were. Ricardo fell over while Shelly lunged at thin air and crashed backwards into the hallway.

Asha switched the EMP timer to "60" and threw it to the back of the room.

"I'm sorry, Drone! I had to!" Asha cried. "Run for the lift!" she yelled at the others, sealing the door with her Superglue Shooter as they escaped. As they ran, Asha could hear Shelly in the distance gasping for breath. She wheezed at Ricardo.

"Do not let them leave without a proper goodbye."

Chapter 17

-.- . . .--. / --. --- .. -. --. -.-.-- / .- .-.. -- ---
... - / - .... . .-. . -.-.--

14:28

Asha and Nush ran straight into the path of three advancing ShellyParrots. Their eyes flashed blue.

"TARGETS IDENTIFIED!" they screeched in unison.

"This way!" yelled Drone. The gang turned, but the corridor was lined on both sides with more parrots. Their beaks swivelled, and they looked straight at the gang. "ATTACK!" they called.

"The dance!" shrieked Asha, bopping her legs and waving her arms. Nush joined in too.

"They'll malfunction in no time," said Asha. A parrot dived at her face and she ducked.

"I don't think it's working, Asha," panicked Nush, spinning away from another attack.

Asha saw a sea of blue eyes flashing. "DANCING IDENTIFIED. TARGETS LOCKED." This time the parrots weren't confused at all.

"Their code's been updated!" cried Asha, casting her eyes around for another escape route.

Nush looked at her sister in amazement. How did she know all of this?

"Over here!" said Drone. They darted round a corner. The parrots were whirring close behind them.

"It feels like we're running in a circle!" Asha yelled. She was right: the corridor curved around on itself. They ran through a set of doors and froze. They were back where they'd started, opposite the lift. DJ-B appeared opposite them, panting.

"I'll stay here and deal with these parrots. Go and do your thing!" DJ-B winked at Nush. "Stay cool, big sis!"

"Thank you!" yelled Asha and Nush, as they bundled back into the lift. "Tumble! Here!" Asha knelt, opened her backpack and Tumble shot in just as the lift doors closed.

DING.

The lift doors opened, and they stepped out into the calm, quiet reception. Asha tried not to breathe too heavily.

"Got everything you need?" said the man behind the desk.

"Yes, thank you," said Nush, cool as a cucumber, as Drone whirred ahead, out into the grey light of the street.

Asha followed Drone out of the building and

blinked her eyes into focus. It seemed crazy that everyone was going about their day as usual, with no idea that Asha and Nush had just escaped an attack from killer parrots.

"Your heart rate is worryingly high, Asha," Drone beeped. "Normally, I would advise that you breathe deeply and slowly. But as you have just dispatched the most lethal gadget in existence, PANICKING IS APPROPRIATE!" Drone's screen started to pixelate.

"Not now, Drone!" Perhaps she shouldn't have used the EMP-Ender, but it was too late to worry about that. Asha was trying to think what to do next, but her thoughts were all jumbled. She hit the CSA button on her watch.

"Hedy, it's Agent Asha reporting in," Asha said, trying to remember if there was a protocol she should be following. "We require assistance, if you don't mind, because we are sort of being chased by a ton of robot parrots, and we really need to—"

"—get out of here!" Nush cried, pointing towards a fleet of four-by-four cars to their right, driving out in a long line from the ShellyPlex.

Asha felt a cool, clammy sweat on her forehead. "Come in, Hedy, please," she whispered into her watch as the big, menacing cars turned towards them. Asha looked up and saw a blue mobile library bus pull up right in front of them. Just in time.

Chapter 18

--. .-. . .- - / .--- --- -... --..-- / .- --. . -. -
-.-.--

14:35

"To the ferry, ASAP! Chalo!" cried Asha, as they
jumped into the back of the library van.

A twinkly old lady turned round from the
driver's seat.

"This isn't a bus, sweetie!" she said. "This
is Booky, the Orkney mobile library! And I'm
Lorraine. It's a pleasure to meet you."

Asha was caught out, for just a second. She'd
only been in self-driving CSA vans before – she
hadn't been expecting a human being! This van
must be an older model.

"Ha! Of course it's just a mobile library..."

Asha winked. "But how do you turn on all the spy gadgets?" Asha tried her CSA Copycat Card on a few of the books without any luck.

Lorraine looked confused for a second, but then she caught Nush's eye and smiled. "With the power of your imagination," said Lorraine, winking back at Asha. "Got a big mind here, don't we!" She nodded at Tumble.

"Yes, my mind is massive!" Tumble replied. "Huge."

Nush grabbed Asha by the elbow and hissed in her ear. "This isn't a spy bus, silly. This is just a normal library bus."

Asha's face fell. Oh no. The four-by-fours were closing in.

"Please can you help?" Asha said. She looked at her watch. She'd set the EMP-Ender nine minutes ago. Only 51 minutes to go before it detonated and possibly killed her two favourite robots in the world. "We need to get to the ferry ASAP, please."

"This is not a taxi!" Lorraine replied.

Nush saw a Save The Planet sticker in the window. "We're on a mission to help save the planet and the world's natural trees. We're investigating the new Cyber Oaks..."

"Oh, those dreaded things." Lorraine paused. "I love nature too. C'mon then, let's go."

"Thank you so much!" said Nush. We need to get to..." She looked at Drone. "St Margaret's Hope," Drone beeped.

"It leaves soon and our parents are waiting for us," continued Nush. She elbowed Asha, and they both turned on their biggest, widest eyes.

"Aye, I know it well." Asha and Nush exchanged a smile. Lorraine turned the bus around, and they bounced off up the road. She put her foot on the gas, headed up over a hill and then turned sharply down a side street. The four-by-fours disappeared from the wing mirror.

Asha pulled out her tablet to check for a signal. Nothing. Asha was trying desperately to check the latest Cyber Oak news, but without any success. She held it to the window. Still nothing.

"Woweee," said Tumble, nose pressed against the rear window. "Look at that!" A huge black four-by-four had sped into view. "Blacked-out windows. Shiny wheels. It looks just like DJ Bestlyfe's car. Wait..." The car had zoomed up behind them and Tumble spotted the number plate. "B LYF3! Guys, it *is* DJ-B!" He reached for his phone to zoom in on the driver. "Oh wait, that's not DJ-B – that's Shelly. Everyone, panic!"

The four-by-four rumbled over the cobbles and

accelerated right up to
their bumper. Ricardo
was at the wheel, with
Shelly in the passenger
seat and Amanda on
her lap, head out of
the window, yapping
at the air.

"Errr," panicked Asha, turning to Lorraine. "I
was wondering if it's possible to go a tiny bit faster."

"What's that, dear? You'll have to speak up. Into
my good ear, now!"

"Can you go any faster?" Asha shouted over the
noise of the bus. Ricardo revved the black car's
engine, swerved left to right and tried to overtake.

The bus lurched to the side. "Oh behave,
laddie," called Lorraine. "You can see I'm a long
vehicle!"

The librarian swung the bus across the road and
turned sharply down a single-track road. "You OK
in the back there? It's gone quiet," said Lorraine.

"All good!" said Nush. Her knuckles turned

white as she held on, while Drone's emergency warning triangle flashed continuously.

Ricardo swung back into view behind them. Asha saw the sign to the ferry. "Not long now, my dears!" called Lorraine.

Drone checked the ferry timetables and calculated the route. "The likelihood of making the ferry is 2.7 per cent." Even worse, the four-by-fours were now approaching from both behind them and ahead.

"We're toast," Asha muttered under her breath.

"Speaking of which, it's time you had a snack," advised Drone.

"Not now, Drone!" Asha was busy thinking.

She had an idea. She took a book off the shelf and rolled down the window. "Nush, grab my waist!" Asha leaned out and flung a book at the four-by-four. It bounced off the bonnet. Useless. She hated destroying books, but this was an emergency. "Pass me a bigger book – much bigger!" she called. Nush hauled the biggest book she could find and handed it over to Asha.

"Perfect!" said Asha, as the road curved and
Ricardo closed in. She hurled the book in a high
arc. Its pages flew open and it landed flat on
the windscreen. Ricardo swerved, skidded and
careered off the road, dodging a stone wall by
millimetres. He crashed through a steel gate and
skidded to a stop in a field.

Lorraine was completely focused on the road
ahead. "Bit draughty in here!" she called back, her
glasses almost flying off her face. "Would you mind
closing the window?" Asha ducked back in and
wound the window up.

Lorraine turned down a side road, accelerated

towards a wall and veered sharp left, before popping out at the ferry car park. "She's still there. That's good. You'll have to jump on quickly and find your folks," she said, skidding to a halt on the dock. A man in a hi-vis vest was just undoing a rope attached to the ferry. Lorraine wound down the window.

"Wee Davie! How's yer mam? Hold it a moment! I've got two bairns for you!" She turned back to the girls. "Go on, he'll hold the boat for you."

"Thank you SO much!" said Asha and Nush together, scrambling out of the van. They ran up the ramp and onto the ferry. The water churned as the engine roared to life, and the ferry began to move. They had made it!

Asha looked back from the deck of the ferry. The black four-by-four had screeched to a halt just a metre from the water. Its doors flew open, and Ricardo and Shelly leapt out.

Across the water, Asha heard Shelly shouting at Ricardo.

"PERHAPS WE'LL LET AMANDA DRIVE NEXT TIME!"

Asha's watch pinged: 15 minutes to go until the vote opened. She connected to the ferry WiFi, and opened up FaceSpace, taking a moment to read back the posts Nush had written about the Cyber Oak. Nush was a great writer.

The truth was out there, and thanks to the spambots it was spreading like wildfire. Asha waited for a moment – then saw it being liked and shared, liked and shared – 20, 200, 2,000, 20,000, 2,000,000 times.

In just 45 minutes, the EMP-ender would detonate and destroy the spambots for good. Shelly wouldn't be able to flood the world with any more fake news, and by that time, the truth would be out there and the gang would be in the middle of the North Sea, far away from harm.

The ferry chugged away and Orkney faded into the distance. Asha's plan had worked.

Chapter 19

-- --- .-. . / -- .. .. --- -. ... / .- / -.-.
... .- / -.. --- - / .-- --- .-. .-.. -.. .-.-.-

August 09 18:13

"We did it!" screamed Tumble, jumping up and punching the air with his tiny fists. "I knew we would! LION!"

The gang huddled around Tumble's tablet. Two glittery presenters were announcing the results of the final.

"MC Dog is all set for mega-stardom and a lifetime supply of dog biscuits," continued Tumble. "It's, like, the best thing that has happened. Ever."

Asha scrunched up her face. Only 24 hours ago, they had saved not only Wembley Park, but all of the trees in the world. Which, to Asha, was actually one of the best things that had ever happened. And now, much to Tumble's extreme joy, MC Dog had won "Show-Off".

Asha flicked the channel to Wolf News, tuning in to the daily round-up.

"In a remarkable turn of events, the residents of Wembley have voted against the introduction of the Cyber Oak to their local park. With just minutes to go before the vote, a whistle-blower released detailed reports that showed years of cover-ups and manipulated climate data, causing a landslide shift in public opinion."

Asha couldn't believe they had pulled it off. Once the truth was out there, everything had happened so quickly. After the ferry, there had been three more train journeys and a motorbike dash to get back to London, and then some serious covering up to do with Mum and Dad. The spambots had helped to spread the real reports on the Cyber Oak at record speed, faster and wider than Asha had ever thought was possible. Even after the bots had been destroyed by the EMP-Ender, the news kept spreading. Reporters all over the world covered the story.

And then the Kenton Broadcasting Cooperation got going. Nani-ji made sure the whole of Wembley, Kenton and beyond knew the truth using her own word-of-mouth network. And they turned out in their thousands to vote "no" to the Cyber Oak.

When the story had broken, Shelly started to dish out denials. She blah-blah-ed on about how much she loved kittens, endangered species and most of all her fan-ily. She claimed not to have known the truth about what was happening, and blamed a bunch of high-profile executives at Shelly Inc.

Now that Asha was home, sitting cross-legged on her bed with Tumble and Drone, it almost felt like a dream. Almost.

"We go live now to Shelly Belly herself," the newsreaders continued.

Shelly's voice oozed into the room. "I was as shocked as all my followers were at this news. Just like you, I was fooled. I've heard from many people who felt hurt by the – lawful – use of FaceSpace to spread disinformation. And I've listened. Shelly Inc has accepted the resignation of its chief information officer, Dr S. Cape-Goat. My heart broke when I heard the truth."

"She's such a liar!" said Asha, speaking over the soundbite.

Shelly's voice persisted. "The truth is important. I love the truth. That's why I've set up an independent inquiry into the Cyber Oak Truth, chaired by me. And from now on, all fake news shared on FaceSpace will be tagged with my latest innovation, the Fake News Fart – available for a small fee of £5.99 a month."

Tumble giggled. "She's so funny," he said.

"Meanwhile, the Council of Nations has awarded Shelly its highest honour: the Order of The Truth," the newsreader concluded.

How does Shelly keep winning awards? Asha thought, amazed. Who gives out these awards? Who judges them? Why are there awards at all? And why can't anyone see that Shelly's just a big liar?

"Boring," said Tumble, flicking to Coyote TV.

The lights in Asha's room suddenly flashed and a large hologram of a squirrel appeared above her bed.

It was Hedy.

"Good evening, Asha. Excellent work on Mission Cyber Oak. You showed a sharp intellect in identifying Shelly's spambots. And your unique skills in solving problems, holding your nerve and acting without self-interest are precisely the qualities we value in our secret agents. Our mission analysis is complete."

Asha beamed. This was the moment she had been waiting for.

"You needed 20 points to pass probation. You accrued 20 on the course of the mission."

Asha jumped from her bed. Finally! She'd made it! She was a fully-fledged member of the CSA.

"However, 35 points were deducted for breaches. Outcome: probation status remains."

"What?" Asha's cheeks were burning, and her shoulders slumped. "But it was a success!"

"You broke several CSA protocols. You removed CSA equipment from the sleeper train without authorization and abandoned most of it in the field. We can't risk gadgets falling into the wrong hands."

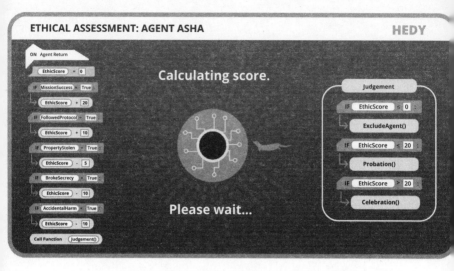

Asha remembered the climbing rope. And she hadn't seen the CSA grappling hook for a while.

"You also revealed sensitive information to your sister, Anushka Joshi, despite our confidentiality protocols."

"Nush helped us!" Asha pleaded. The probation algorithm just didn't feel fair.

"You also ignored our very clear warning and used a lethal weapon without permission," said Hedy.

"Yes, I know ... but it did say that the EMP-Ender should only be used in extreme circumstances, and this was a big-time emergency!" Asha protested.

"We require complete honesty from our agents.

Had we known, we would have issued guidance on the most appropriate settings. Instead, you had the EMP on its most powerful setting, and wiped out all of the computers on the island, causing extreme disruption to innocent lives."

"But..."

"This is a Class A Breach," Hedy continued matter-of-factly.

Asha's heart sank. She clicked on the assessment and looked through the CSA's decision-making flowchart. She had passed the mission except for the Class A Breach.

"You have great potential, Asha. I am confident you will grow to become an accomplished CSA agent. We'll see you at circus school in the summer."

Asha barely heard the last words. The bottom of her screen flashed with messages from agents congratulating her on completing her mission. She even got a message from Agent Tyler in California, who spent most of his time at the bottom of the sea. Asha was happy that the mission had been a success. She had protected the environment from a global threat. And she would still be able to climb and fall off trees in Wembley Park. But – she couldn't help it – she still felt like she'd failed.

They were interrupted by a warning from Drone. "Your sister is about to enter."

"I'll be back," Asha told Hedy, as she enabled Pizza Mode. Once again, her room transformed into her normal bedroom: tools, empty crisp packets and socks all over the floor.

"My little spy hero!" Nush exclaimed as she barged in. "Ew, what's that smell?"

"Anushka Avani Joshi," Hedy boomed, overriding Pizza Mode.

"I'm here," said Nush, frowning and mouthing, "*Really?*" at Asha.

"Anushka, on behalf of the CSA, I wish to commend you for exceptional spy-like conduct. You would make an excellent CSA agent, should you wish to join."

Asha looked up, aghast. This was too much.

"Oh, thank you. But I need to focus on my

music right now." Nush smiled at her sister. "Plus, you can't really have two spies in the same house."

"Understood. Small talk over. Keep safe." There was a *zap* and Hedy was gone.

Nush turned to Asha. Nush could always tell if the smallest thing was wrong, almost like she had a sixth sense. "What's up, Sis?"

"Nothing. It's just that I'm still on CSA spy probation. And #AshaPoopyPants is still trending, and it's not the spambots any more."

Nush had taken a seat next to her sister on the end of her bed. "Those people on FaceSpace don't know you. But I do. You're kind, brave and smart. You uncovered the truth about the Cyber Oak, you stood up to the world's most powerful entrepreneur and you never gave up, not even once."

Nush put her arm around Asha and gave her a squeeze. "You're amazing, Ashypoo. And you always have, and always will be able to do, the most powerful farts on this planet. It's a pure gift."

"Sniff, sniff, hmmff." Tumble was dramatically wiping his eyes with a hankie. "You guys!" He winked at Drone. "Play it!"

The familiar beat of MC Dog's "Winner" played, and Tumble rapped over the top.

Yo yo yo, I'm the Tee-Tumble-Eee.
Other toy hamsters been looking at me.

Nush snorted. Asha slowly began to smile. Tumble grabbed a pen lid as a microphone, and pranced up and down the desk in time to the music.

I snap selfies at breakfast
And I always vlog my lunch.
Parrot bots see me dancing
And their code gets in a crunch.
When we found out the truth,
It was hard-hitting stuff.
We saved the trees and won the vote –
It wasn't good enough.

So Asha's really sad now.
She's still on probation.
Gotta wait till next time
For that big celebration!
There is some good news
So you don't need to cry.
After circus school this summer
She will be a MEGA spy!

Nush whooped as Drone fanned Tumble with her propeller. Asha's mind raced over the events of the last few days. She had been on a zip line, ferry and overnight train, argued with a talking tree, been chased by killer parrots and escaped who-knows-what in a getaway vehicle. Asha was still desperate to pass her probation. But there was time for that. And she'd done something really important for the planet.

Asha was proud of herself.

"GIRLS. DINNER!" Mum yelled.

Asha grinned and hopped off the bed.

"COMING!"

Epilogue

August 10 - 02:46

She had tried everything:
doctors, gurus, spiritual
healers, restrictive diets and
sleeping with an octopus on
her face. She'd bought a farm in
Wales so she could count real sheep
through a webcam. But nothing worked.
Shelly could not get to sleep at night. Her
mind raced. Numbers floated and glowed in front
of her: her bank balance, her health data and –
most important – the number of people who used
FaceSpace daily.

Shelly changed position again. She tried her bedtime mantras: "Breathe in success. Breathe out unpopularity. Breathe in likes. Breathe out unfollows." She began to relax. She felt a heaviness in her arms.

Then it hit her. She couldn't avoid the memory any longer.

The playground. Shelly in the corner. Giti and Shelly holding hands.

Shelly felt a sob growing in her throat. *Where was Giti now?* she thought. Why hadn't Shelly been able to find her? Almost every single person on the planet used FaceSpace, or knew someone who did. Shelly could discover what anyone was doing at any given moment. And yet, there was no sign of Giti.

Shelly turned on her side and stuck a leg out from under the covers. They were tailor-made and precision-engineered, but they still couldn't get her temperature just right. Yet another disappointment.

Images of Asha flashed before her eyes. That little cutie had given her the first flicker of competition she'd felt in a while. It was a shame about the trees. But of course, Asha hadn't really won – Shelly had already started planning her next invention, Cyber Dirt. It was even more powerful than the Cyber Oak. Still, Shelly admired Asha's tenacity, if nothing else. Maybe she should hire her. Teach her a few things. It would be a chance to exploit her skills.

Shelly sat up. It was no use. She'd never get to sleep now. She reached for her tablet, opened a new email and began to type.

<Case file>   <Suspect file>   <Fake news>   <Top secret>   <Missions>

CASE FILE:
ASHA JOSHI

Name: Asha Joshi

Age: 11 years old

Status: Agent [ON PROBATION]

Current location: London, UK

Recorded data:

Location:
Wembley,
London, UK

3
Agility level

Completed missions:
Mission Shark Bytes
Operation Cyber Chop

Psychological profile:

- Rebellious
- Doesn't trust authority figures
- Not keen on following orders

Skills:

- Coding
- Crafts and robotics
- Bravery
- Cyber Security Specialist
  Can hack into remote accounts

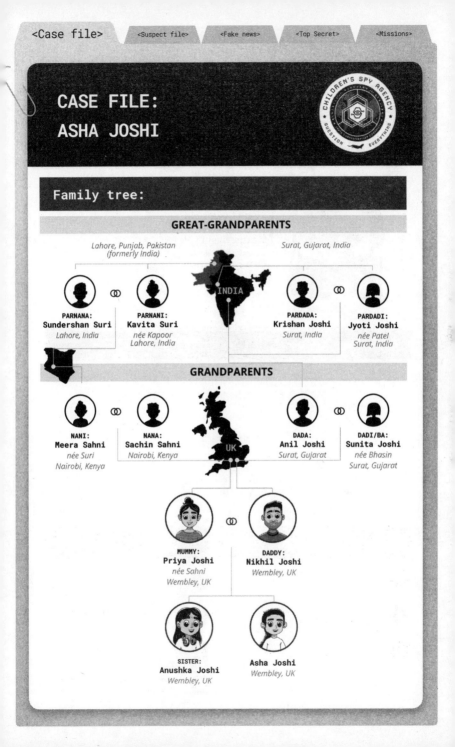

<Case file>   <Suspect file>   <Fake news>   <Top secret>   <Missions>

CASE FILE:
ANUSHKA JOSHI

Name: Anushka Joshi

Age: 14 years old

Status: Potential agent

Current location: London, UK

Recorded data:

While not an expert in traditional spycraft skills, Agent Asha's older sibling demonstrated highly developed EQ and commitment to CSA values. Could be recruited.

2

EQ
level

Other skills:

      /

- Music composition and production
- Online content
- Creative writing

 EQ, also called emotional intelligence (EI), measures a person's ability to understand and control their feelings, and to interact with others through being sensitive to their emotions.

<Suspect file>   <Case file>   <Fake news>   <Top secret>   <Missions>

SUSPECT: SHELLY BELLY

Name: Shelly Belly

Age: 17 years old

FaceSpace followers: 108.4 million

Current location: London, UK

Recorded data:

- Suspect of the CSA
- Social media celebrity, tech entrepreneur
- Second richest person on the planet

Unethical actions:

 Owns all copyright to every picture uploaded on her apps.

Punishes employees for toilet breaks over 5 minutes.

 Tried to take over the Internet.

Seems to be above legal repurcussions?

<Suspect file>   <Case file>   <Fake news>   <Top secret>   <Missions>

SUSPECT:
RICARDO KON CARNEY

Name: Ricardo Kon Carney

Age: 19 years old

Status: PR Manager

Current location: London, UK

Psychological profile:

Workaholic, craves validation from Shelly Belly. Has a cruel streak and takes out anger on employees.

Recorded data:

- Puts Shelly's needs over own safety and wellbeing.

- Will follow Shelly's orders even when they are irrational and go against good judgement.

- Averages five hours sleep each night. Effects include impaired reaction time, rash decision making, bad mood.

SUSPECT

<Suspect file> <Case file> <Fake news> <Top secret> <Missions>

SUSPECT: RICARDO KON CARNEY

CHILDREN'S SPY AGENCY
QUESTION EVERYTHING

Media:

Ricardo Follow ···

362 likes

Got Swag. #ifyouknowyouknow#iykyk

Tabletop RPG character. Level 12 Human Barbarian named Rik Aah'Do The Smasher

21:18 85%

Chattr

Ricardo Kon Carney
@Taking-the-rick Today at 1.13 PM

Cyber oak haters are so basic. Shelly's a genius queen who opened a micro-pig sanctuary and made a million quid this morning. What did *you* do this morning?

Ricardo Kon Carney
@Taking-the-rick Today at 9.35 AM

You know baristas spell your name wrong on cups on purpose so you'll photograph it and put it on social media.

> Reply
Today at 9.35 AM

WAIT I TOTALLY JUST DID IT THO

Ricardo Kon Carney
@Taking-the-rick Yesterday at 6.00 AM

Happy Birthday to Parrot Drone P47-0002 (I call her Pat 2). I figure since hardware has a lifespan of about 7 years, 10 human years = 1 drone year, so being 36.4 days old is basically like being a year old for a drone. #JustNerdyThings

> Reply from @RealShellyB
Rickybae, it's 6 AM, what on earth are you talking about?

INTERNAL USE ONLY

<Missions>   <Suspect file>   <Fake news>   <Top secret>   <Case file>

CSA BRIEFING:
OPERATION CYBER CHOP

Fake news:

Fake news is when people share things online as "facts" that are untrue or misleading. Fake news is bad because it may make people believe things that aren't true, but also because it makes them sceptical about whether they can trust scientists or other sources of reliable information.

Types of fake news:

Disinformation

Fake stories deliberately spread by people who know they're fake to hurt people they don't like, or get them attention.

Example

People often edit photos and videos to make it look like they caught a UFO on camera because it gets them a lot of attention. Lots of people are fooled by these.

<Missions> <Suspect file> <Fake news> <Top secret> <Case file>

CSA BRIEFING:
OPERATION CYBER CHOP

Misinformation

Fake stories spread by people who don't know they're false and think they're being helpful.

Example

About twelve million people believe that the world is secretly ruled by alien shape-shifting lizard-people, and that many famous singers, actors and politicians are actually lizard people disguised as humans. They believe this is 100 per cent real and that you need to know about it.

Warning: confirmation bias!

Everyone is more likely to believe things that support what they already believe, even CSA agents. We're more likely to believe things we hear from people we like, even if they're not experts in what they're talking about. This is called "confirmation bias".

We encourage all agents to look into things for themselves. Check the source, the date and if other sources say the same thing before sharing news online.

CHECKLIST

- [x] The news is from a respected site or person.
- [x] Other respected sites and people say the same thing.
- [ ] It's recent.

TUMBLE'S CHEEKY ♡ ♡ GUIDE TO FARMING

So, like, here's the scenario. You want to make a whole lot of a thing. Maybe it's clicks, maybe it's sweet, sweet corn (om nom nom). You can do it with this one WEIRD TRICK!

STARRING TUMBLE!

HYPE!

A + MEME

FARMING.

It's where you get a place or a bunch of people and just focus on making a thing.

Things you can farm:

Plant, Egg and Animal Farms

Agricultural farms are, like, SO basic. Existed before they even invented WiFi! Involves wellies and mud. HARD PASS.

NO

Click Farms

Posts not going viral? Big mood. Some cheaters use click farms: offices where people click on ads or share posts all day. Don't do this. Click farms treat their workers badly, don't pay well and sometimes break laws!

Server Farms

The internet is just a bunch of computers wired up, so you need a place to keep them all that's nice and chill. Under water or in, like ... idk, Siberia.

BRRRR

17:15 WARNING 001

Always be on the lookout for disguised cameras. People have found cameras disguised as USB chargers, fire alarms, air fresheners and even bottles of water!

19:02 INTEL 012

You can check where a smart speaker or news feed is getting its news from in the settings, and customise which sources you would like it to use.

19:08 WARNING 002

In 2016, the Natural Environment Research Council launched an online poll to decide the name of a research ship, and the winner was "Boaty McBoatFace". Be careful what you put to an online vote!

21:20 INTEL 014

The famous quote "A lie gets halfway around the world before the truth has a chance to get its pants on" is often attributed to Winston Churchill or Mark Twain, but while both of them did say something like that, neither invented it. That's actually a lie. Ironic!

21:15 INTEL 013

Most of the air on this planet is actually composed of nearly 80% nitrogen. We need oxygen to breathe, but it only makes up roughly 21% of the atmosphere.

80% nitrogen

21% oxygen

21:17 INTEL 015

It is estimated that it will take until 2045 for Artificial Intelligence to be smarter than a human brain.

21:23 INTEL 016

Photos can be artificially altered to mislead people online. Sometimes a photo is used from another event, or the image is cut to change how it appears. Sometimes people will alter photos using image editing software to change things like slogans on signs, make a person look smaller, bigger, angry, happy or even to make it appear that somebody is present who was never really there...

21:31 INTEL 017

While trees are extremely important for oxygen production, it's important to look after the oceans too. A lot of the oxygen on earth is generated by tiny water-dwelling organisms called plankton.

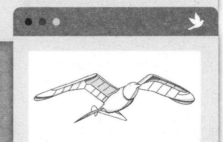

09:04 INTEL 019

Robotics engineers have managed to create robots that fly like real birds by flapping their wings. The robots need to be extremely lightweight (weighing about as much as a hen's egg) to be able to fly.

21:33 INTEL 018

Health and Safety Alert! Goo removed from carpet. Recommend carpet shampoo within the next 3 days.

09:06 INTEL 020

"Clicktivist" is a name for an online activist who shares posts and clicks to sign online petitions but does not do much else to help.

10:15 INTEL 022

The most retweeted tweet on record as of 2022 was by Japanese billionaire Yusaku Maezawa in 2019. It was a money giveaway and got 4.1 million shares.

10:22 INTEL 023

Not all social media bots are bad. Some of them create pleasant artwork like @softlandscapes and others automatically tweet interesting photos from scientific or historical collections, like @the_ephemerides or @museumBot

10:27 INTEL 024

In 2019, the celebrity with the most bot followers was Ellen Degeneres, with 77 million followers. It was estimated that as many as 48% were bots. That's almost half of them!

10:11 INTEL 021

The roar of a lion can be heard as far as 8 kilometres away!

11:43 INTEL 025

Everyone's voice is completely unique, like a fingerprint – even identical twins – so faking a voice to say things the person didn't say can be harder than faking that person's face (which can be reconstructed using a 3D scan).

11:44 WARNING 003

3D-modelling can be used in films to do things like make an actor look younger or even to have a dead actor continue to play a character, so as the technology improves, it could absolutely be used to create fake footage where people appear to do things they never actually did.

21:16 INTEL 026

The Caledonian Sleeper covers over 500 miles, which is a large distance, but nothing compared to the Trans-Siberian Railway, which runs from the east end to the west end of Russia; over 5,000 miles. Riding the full length of this line takes a whole week!

21:41 INTEL 027

Sidonglobophobia is the fear of cotton wool.

22:02 WARNING 004

It is illegal to make EMPs, or Electromagnetic pulse generators, in most countries. They disrupt electronics by creating a surge of energy that can damage circuits and wipe computer memory.

22:04 WARNING 005

The blue light from a screen stops your body creating a chemical, called melatonin, that makes you feel sleepy. Using a phone or tablet an hour or less before bedtime will make it harder to get a good night's sleep.

07:54 INTEL 030

In 2015, British Newspaper the *Sun* used an image of politician Ed Miliband eating a bacon sandwich messily as their front page the day before a national election where he was running for prime minister. Making somebody look ugly, clumsy or awkward is a common tactic to undermine their message.

07:43 INTEL 028

Evidence has been found that suggests humans have been living on Orkney for over 6,500 years.

07:51 INTEL 029

Orkney sheep have evolved to eat a diet of mostly seaweed. Eating too much grass can be bad for some of the sheep, so there has to be a special wall to keep them from eating it.

14:26 INTEL 031

Microsoft's test of the first underwater data centre was successful. The data centre was powered by 100% renewable energy and required very little energy to run.

14:33 WARNING 006

Choosing just the data that backs up what you want people to think is true and ignoring the rest is called "cherry picking". Always look out for it; it's not as delicious as it sounds.

18:08 INTEL 036

Humans, beware. When passing along information the old fashioned way, with telephones or in person, be aware that the message might change after it has been passed along a number of times, as individual humans often mishear or misremember a message before passing it on.

14:37 INTEL 033

In military and spy contexts, "ASAP", which stands for "As soon as possible", is said like "Ay-sap", not "Ay-ess-ay-pee".

WELL DONE.
IF YOU CAN READ THIS YOU'VE
ALREADY PASSED YOUR FIRST TEST.
GO TO WWW.CSA.WORLD/MIRROR
TO START YOUR AGENT TRAINING
OR SCAN THIS QR CODE.

JOIN US
www.csa.world